Virtual Game

By R. L. Copple

Book Three of The Virtual Chronicles

Published by Ethereal Press.
http://www.etherealpress.com

ISBN: 978-0615923741

Prologue

Jeremy stared blankly at the video screens stretching across the Titan station's wall as they scanned Earth's video feeds for crimes in progress. Glimpses of Christmas trees flashed across them as the world he called home, almost a billion miles away, prepared for Christmas the next morning.

"BJ, do you think we'll see Santa from here?" Bridget turned to watch Jeremy's eyes.

He barely cracked a smile. That would certainly get his mind off all the events of the past year. "No, Sis, I seriously doubt it." Jeremy met her eyes. Her short, brown hair brushed her shoulders. "Santa operates under the radar."

She huffed. "You make him sound like a bad guy."

"He does break into people's houses."

She slapped his arm. "To give stuff, not take it."

Jeremy's gut sank. "Christmas did take my life from me. From us." A year ago, he had a normal life. All gone now. All because he had received that stupid helmet for Christmas, had put it on, had become involved with another world's battle, then had become the hero who saved Zoir, SuPuten, and Earth. A year later, his parents dead, the world moved on as if nothing had happened. Another Christmas had come. This time without the Mind Game, but he still had the hero game going.

She slumped in her seat. "I was trying not to think about that."

"Hey, Bucko."

Jeremy swung around. "Hey, Mick. What took you?"

"Family returned late from a Christmas Eve service. Said I wanted to go to bed right away, like I couldn't wait until tomorrow." He smiled. "But I don't have to."

Jeremy raised an eyebrow. "What do you mean, you don't have to wait?"

Mickey slapped Jeremy on the back. "Because I have Astro Man right here. Just use that x-ray beam of yours and I'll know what my presents are tonight!"

Jeremy shook his head. "Mick, you're crazy."

"Oh, come on. I'm hoping they snagged the latest game—"

Jeremy jumped out of his seat. "Another game? Are you crazy?"

Mickey grimaced. "Bucko, what's the deal. It's just a video game."

Jeremy rubbed his forehead. "That's what we thought last year. Just a game. A game that stole my life from me."

Mickey's eyes grew wide. "Ah, of course. Christmas would be triggery for you. I'm sorry."

Jeremy sucked in a deep breath. "Forget it, Mick. It's all I can think about right now."

"What you need is some action. Anything on the vids tonight?"

Jeremy shook his head. "Christmas Eve is pretty quite all over the world it seems."

"Santa." Bridget's voice rang out.

Jeremy spun around. "What?"

She pointed at a video screen. "There's Santa. And he's breaking into a house."

Mickey slapped his hands together. "There's our action. Let's take down Santa."

Jeremy held up a hand. "Mick, this is suspicious. Think about it. How would a live camera crew know about a break-in to a home as it happens and be there to record it?"

Mickey shrugged. "Happened to be in the right place at the right time? They've probably called the cops, but are filming it for the drama."

"Maybe." Jeremy stared at it a bit longer. "Aren't there movie plots about Santa stealing things?" Micky stared at him. Jeremy called out, "Computer, find movies where Santa steals." A screen went blank and then a list of titles appeared. The highest rated link read, "The Adventure of the Wrong Santa Claus" in 1914. Related links followed it.

Mickey read the results. "Are you saying the Zorians are behind this? Else I'm not following you. Santa thieves have been around forever."

"Yes . . .I mean, no. I doubt it is a Zorian. But it still makes me suspicious."

"Okay, so maybe it's a trap. Maybe it's not. And if it's not, guess who loses?"

Jeremy ran his fingers through his hair. "Yes, you're right. But stay together. My gut is saying something is wrong here."

"Agreed," Mickey responded.

Bridget jumped from the chair. "Sure, but we'll be virtual. We can't get hurt."

Jeremy stood. "Then as you say, Mick, let's do this."

Mickey grinned. "This will be good for you. You'll see."

Jeremy entered the coordinates. "Suit, appear as Astro Man."

The room faded and a breeze blew across his chin extending from below his helmet. The half-moon cast a dim glow over the residential neighborhood. A street light flickered a few yards to the right. Activity buzzed to his left where a camera crew recorded the house, waiting for the thief to exit. A siren blared in the distance, indicating the police were indeed on their way. Mickey was probably right. They would save someone's Christmas from being stolen and save Christmas for some kids.

Mickey appeared beside him as Blue Nova. Jeremy could barely make out the blue-green suit, blue briefs, and dark blue cape in the moonlight.

Bridget materialized as Rainbow Girl to his left. Her sparkly mask flaring at the end reflected the meager light.

Jeremy caught her eye. "Rainbow Girl?"

She smiled. "You catch 'em. I'm make 'em cooperative."

Jeremy nodded. "Sounds like a plan. You stay out here. Blue Nova and I will grab this guy." He turned toward Mickey. "I'll use my light-flash on my gun, and while the crew is blinded, race in there and grab him, bring him to Rainbow Girl, and she'll make him giddy with cooperation."

Mickey saluted. "Sir, yes, sir!"

"Mick!"

"Lighten up, Bucko. Have a little fun with this. You're way too wound up."

Jeremy unsheathed his gun and set it for a light blast. "You should never let your guard down. Assume nothing."

"It's just a lone Santa thief. What could go wrong?"

"I hope you're right." Jeremy pointed the gun toward the camera crew. "Hide your eyes. On three. One, two, three!" Jeremy squeezed the trigger and a blast of light lit up the area. The camera crew rubbed their eyes and swore in the quiet neighborhood. Within a second, Mickey flashed back with a squirming man in his arms. Mickey dropped him on the ground.

"What the—" The man's eyes darted around.

Bridget extended her arms and flow of rainbow colors enveloped the man.

Santa's eyes blinked and a grin spread across his face. "So much for my Christmas. But that's okay. I'm happy anyway."

Jeremy pointed to the street. "Go sit on the curb and wait for the police. Give yourself up when they arrive."

"Oh gladly I will. I was so bad to try and steal . . . you."

Jeremy's eyes widened. "What did you say?"

The back of the news van flung open. A line of soldiers carrying automatic rifles streamed out the door. Jeremy raised his gun to set it for shields, but before he could, a rain of bullets spread over them. He could feel the bullets hitting him. He would have called out to exit the suit, but dying in the virtual body would accomplish the same thing. This did appear to be a trap, but what trap? They would wake up and come back again. Apparently they didn't know much about how virtual bodies worked. But why did the army set this trap?

As life ebbed from the virtual body, Mickey dropped out of nova speed and fell to the ground. He hadn't reacted fast enough, despite his super speed. Jeremy crumbled onto the grass as blackness swept over him.

———

Jeremy jerked his eyes open. He tried to focus, but the ceiling he saw was not the stucco of his uncle's house at the top of a Montana mountain. Instead, polished metal greeted his eyes. He pushed himself up.

Thick hands wrapped around his arms and another pulled the cowl off his head. "Commander, Operation Christmas Gift has been completed, sir."

Jeremy groaned inwardly. Their bodies had been captured while they were virtual. Two men on either side of him kept a firm grip on his arms, another two stood toward the foot of his bed, rifles aimed at the floor, ready to use. No doubt another two stood behind him.

A higher ranking solider beside his bed examined the cowl. "Very interesting. I'm sure our scientist will have a field day with this."

Jeremy struggled to speak through a dry throat. "Earth's best scientist couldn't figure out how the Mind Game helmets operated. What makes you think this will be easier?"

A smug smile creased his lips. "We've actually made progress in figuring out the helmets. But we're missing a point of reference."

Jeremy squinted at him. "What?"

"Point of reference. The helmets, as you know, don't work. And even when they did, the destination was in another galaxy. But with these in hand and the destination being in the same room, they'll be able to trace the energy field being created, and hopefully come up with the remaining pieces of the puzzle."

Jeremy let himself fall back to the cot. The soldier's hands loosened but remained firm. "No one can use the mask but me. Same with the other mask Mickey and Bridget have. They are programmed to respond only to our voices."

The man shot a stare at Jeremy. "You'll forgive me if I don't trust you."

"Be my guest." Jeremy turned to meet his eyes. "But how did you find us?"

He waved his hand. "Simple deduction. When the superhero appearances began to be reported all over the world, and your friend and sister's personas helped in defending Earth from the Similarians, it became obvious that the same virtual reality of the Mind Game was at work. From there you were the most logical culprits. We tracked down your locations and set the trap to grab you."

Jeremy stared at the wall. He should have foreseen this possibility. "Why, though? Why revert to kidnapping us?"

The soldier stuffed the cowl into his pocket. "Control, Jeremy Goodhue. We like to have control over situations. And I didn't suspect you'd approve of us gaining that control. But if we can duplicate this technology, our forces would be invincible. We can fight wars on the ground without losing a life. With a legion of virtual Blue Novas to speed in and hit the enemy before they even blink, we could maintain control for decades. Centuries even. Can you imagine the progress? Can you see the peace we could uphold?"

Jeremy knew he didn't want to tell the man anything else. Let him think he could succeed. As soon as the Zorians caught wind of it, they'd shut off the virtual energy going through the wormhole and that would be that. No more superhero days for himself, Mickey, and Bridget. Then again, that didn't sound so bad. He wouldn't mind putting the whole thing behind him and salvage what he could of his life.

"Peace?" Jeremy breathed deep. "By killing?"

He smiled. "Youthful idealism. I'm afraid the world is a dangerous place. Some people only understand one thing. Brut force."

Jeremy grumbled under his breath, "That's what all bullies think."

"What?" The Commander stared at him for a couple of seconds. Then turned and headed for the door. He paused as he opened it. "By the way. Merry Christmas, Jeremy." He left and shut the door behind him.

Jeremy groaned. *We may have killed Rillian, but his spirit lives on.*

———

The Commander returned to the room after an hour had passed. His lips down-turned, he faced Jeremy lying on the bed. "You were right. We have to use you to get the mask to operate. Come with me." He turned on his heels and headed to the door.

Arms pulled Jeremy off the bed. He stumbled along beside the soldiers as they exited the room and marched down the hall. The Commander stopped in front of a door and pointed at the window.

Jeremy moved to look in, keeping his eyes fixed on the Commander's stoic gaze. He peered in. Uncle George sat on a cot, wearing coveralls and a hat as if they'd snatched him while he milked the cows.

"Just want to ensure your cooperation. If you resist or try anything foolish, it won't go well for your uncle, sister, or friend."

Jeremy met his gaze. "We're United States citizens. What about our constitutional rights to due process? You can't threaten us like this."

A smile cracked on his lips. "To the government, the Congress, and the Constitution, we don't exist. You'll have a hard time suing an organization that doesn't exist."

"How do I know you have my sister and friend?"

The Commander nodded down the hall. They stopped at the next two cell doors. Bridget sat on the cot rocking her feet under it. Mickey circled his cot as if deep in thought. "Satisfied?"

Jeremy nodded and followed the soldiers down the hall, a right turn into another hall, a left, and a few doors on the right, they entered a room. Waist-high tables lined the walls. Chairs sat scattered in front of them where soldiers worked on different projects. Centrifuges, Bunsen burners, test tubes, microscopes, and various other lab equipment littered the table-tops.

In the center of the room stood a dentist-like chair fastened with heart monitors, IVs, and a foil ring that swiveled off the top of the chair's back, as if it would fit on someone's head. A movable light hovered over the chair. The light probably wasn't to get a better view of one's mouth.

The soldiers jumped to their feet as the Commander strolled to the center of the room. He patted the chair. "Lay down here."

Jeremy didn't see he had any other option. So he crawled into the chair and laid his head against the back. Jeremy watched as the Commander reached onto the table where a soldier stood at attention, and picked up his cowl. Bridget's and Mickey's masks had lain beside it.

The Commander held the mask in front of Jeremy. "You will put this on, then appear in this room as one of your characters. If you do not appear here, I will order the termination of one of those we are holding."

Jeremy's jaw dropped. "Murder?" He had to be bluffing.

"Oh, it would be an accident. Your Uncle falls off the mountain. Your sister drowns in a lake. Your friend shows up in an automobile accident while walking home. All after we terminate them and plant the evidence. We could even implicate you in their deaths if we wished. Now you don't want their blood on your hands, do you?"

"Investigators would know we didn't die that way." Jeremy gritted his teeth. "You couldn't get away with it!"

The Commander stared into Jeremy's eyes. "We have, we are, and we will again. Now are we clear?"

Jeremy bored into the Commander's eyes. If

the man was bluffing, he couldn't tell. Nor could he take the chance he wasn't. "You're clear. I'll cooperate."

"Good." He handed Jeremy the cowl.

Jeremy slipped it over his head and leaned back. The ring was snuggled down upon his head. He whispered in hopes they wouldn't pick up the words, but the mask would. "Suit, appear here as Astro Man."

The room dimmed, then reappeared, except now he stood to the side of the chair watching his body breathe in front of him. Feet scurried behind him. "Hand's up!"

Jeremy raised his hands. Fingers wrapped around his gun and then yanked it from its holster. The soldier held the raygun in his hand. A slight smile spread over the man's lips.

Jeremy nodded at the gun. "Careful with that, dude. Whatever you do, don't pull the trigger."

The Commander jumped to the soldier and pulled it from his hands. He turned it over as he examined it. "Why? What would happen."

Jeremy forced a grin to stay hidden. "Trust me. The last thing you want to do is pull that trigger."

The Commander continued to scan the gun. "Sargent, start the energy trace from the body to the virtual body."

"Sir, yes, sir." Several of the men turned back to their work.

The Commander lifted the gun's barrel and rested it over his extended left arm. He pointed it at the far wall where a two-feet thick, titanium, three by three foot wall stood. A blackened area covered the center of the metal wall as if lasers had hit it countless times.

"Sir, do you think that is a good idea? We should interrogate the prisoner first to know what it does."

The Commander turned and stared at the officer for a long five seconds before responding. "You're out of line, soldier. This is a raygun. This dial on top sets the strength. Anyone can see that."

The soldier shrank back to his table. Another officer called out, "Yes, sir. But I saw—"

The Commander ignored the officer and pulled the trigger. The last setting Jeremy had used being the light blast with the camera crew, a blinding light filled the room. Rifles clattered to the floor as everyone hid their eyes.

Jeremy, protected by his helmet's visor, dove to his raygun falling from the Commander's hand, caught it in midair, spun around, and landed on his back. He flipped the gun to the stun ray before anyone could regain their sight and spun himself around on the floor, dropping everyone in the room with a series of thuds and clanks.

"Suit, appear here as Inviso Dude." The room darkened and returned with the bluish glow of the invisibility field. He leaped to his feet, grabbed Bridget and Mickey's mask from the table, then scooped up his own body lying in the chair and flopped it over his shoulder. "Man, I've got to lose some weight."

Jeremy stopped by the Commander's unconscious body. "I told you, you didn't want to pull that trigger." Did the Commander ever read *Briar Rabbit*. He thanked God that the Commander was numbered among the men who didn't think they needed to read the instructions.

With the invisibility field cloaking both his virtual and real body, he stepped through the wall, down the hallway, and into Mickey's cell. He pulled Mickey's mask from his pocket and threw it onto the cot.

Mickey stopped his pacing and jumped. "What the . . ." His eyes widened. "Bucko?"

"Put it on, Mick, grab your body once you've gone virtual, and then hold onto me. I'll extend the invisibility shield around you so we can walk through the wall."

Mickey flopped onto his cot and yanked the mask on. "Suit, appear here as Blue Nova." Blue Nova materialized beside the cot. He pulled his body onto his shoulder, grabbed hold of Jeremy's arm, and became invisible. Jeremy headed for the wall and they stepped into Bridget's cell.

"Sis, put this on." He threw her mask onto the cot. She smiled and jumped up clapping. She put on the mask and became Comet Girl. Jeremy knelt down and pulled Bridget's limp body onto his other shoulder. "Hold onto me everyone. We have one more person to get." They walked through the next wall and into Uncle George's cell. Uncle George latched onto the chain of people. The energy drain on Jeremy caused him to wobble. "Quick, though this door. I can't hold the field much longer."

Jeremy focused on energizing the field as they entered the hallway. They released Jeremy, causing Bridget, Uncle George, and Mickey holding his own body to become visible again. Jeremy breathed easier.

Mickey glanced down each hallway. "Now how do we get out of here? Wherever here is."

The sound of footsteps sounded down the hallway. Jeremy frowned though no one could see it. "I think they've discovered my breakout. Mick, give me your body and do a quick recon. Knock out the soldiers coming and find out where the way out is."

"Your wish is my command." He slipped his body to Jeremy, who piled it on top of his own. Jeremy thanked Holbreth for giving Inviso Dude super human strength.

Mickey sped away into a blur. Jeremy motioned to the rest. "Follow me this way. Comet Girl, scatter some knockout comet dust behind us. Mickey won't be affected by it because he's going too fast."

She nodded. "One dose of sleeping dust, coming up." As Jeremy led Uncle George down the hall away from the coming boots, Bridget extended her hand and scattered dust into the air as she walked backwards.

Sounds of grunts and guns clattering to the floor echoed down the hall. Jeremy doubted they ever saw Blue Nova hit them. Uncle George glanced back. "Is he all right?"

"He's fine. Don't worry about him." Jeremy rounded a corner to find four soldiers pointing rifles at them. Before Bridget could follow him, Jeremy yelled, "Back!" Bullets whizzed harmlessly through him. "Comet Girl, send dust this way."

Bridget stuck her hands around the corner and showered the men with dust. They collapsed onto the floor. Jeremy said, "It's clear." The pair followed him again.

A steel door loomed in front of them. A blue streak stopped in front of Jeremy and Blue Nova appeared. "It must be this way. I checked a few hundred bunk rooms, eating rooms, bathrooms, rec rooms, laboratories, cells, etc., and they were all dead ends."

"Very well." Jeremy stepped through the door and examined the area beyond it. A hanger greeted him dotted with jets. Multiple soldiers worked on the aircraft and guarded the area. A big door that Jeremy bet led outside stood on one side of the massive walls.

Jeremy stepped back into the hallway. "This is certainly the way out. But there are a lot of soldiers on the other side of this door. I'll step you through, Blue Nova, then you can take out as many as possible while I break a hole through this door and we can escape."

Mickey nodded. "Let's do this."

Jeremy held onto Mickey's shoulder until he was through the door, then released him. He watched a moment as Mickey zoomed from person to person, knocking them out with a hit to the head. Jeremy pulled back into the hallway.

Jeremy lay the bodies in a corner. "Suit, appear here as Astro Man." The hallway faded to black immediately returned, but seen through the visor of his helmet. "Stand back, you two." He reached for his gun.

"Halt!" the Commander's voice rang out.

Jeremy jerked his head around. His gut twisted at the sight. The Commander stood, arms crossed, surrounded by ten soldiers pointing rifles at Bridget, himself, and Uncle George.

"Deactivate your virtual personas now, or I'll fire on your uncle." The Commander's eyes bore down upon Jeremy, daring him to disobey.

Jeremy glanced at Uncle George. Uncle George stared at the rifles with wide eyes and backed up against the wall. Jeremy checked on Bridget. She'd closed her eyes and bowed her head as if admitting defeat. There was no way he could pull his gun fast enough to initiate the force field before they pulled the trigger. And Blue Nova, trapped on the other side of the door, couldn't help either.

"Now, Jeremy!" The Commander lifted his hand to give the order.

Jeremy held up a hand. "Okay, you win." He breathed deep. "Suit—"

A blast of light filled the small hallway. A force knocked Jeremy off his feet. His helmet's visor protected him from the light, but he flew through the air, slammed against the wall and crumbled to the floor. The helmet had protected his head from serious injury, but pain roaring through him said otherwise. The force rebounding off the door smashed into Jeremy's body and shoved him ten feet across the hall. Every bone in his body ached, and he could barely move.

"BJ, I mean, Astro Man, are you all right?"

A hand touched his head. He cracked an eye open to see a blurry Comet Girl standing over him. "Was that you?"

"Uh huh. Sorry I couldn't protect you, but I felt keeping a protecting field over Uncle George and our bodies was more important."

Jeremy nodded. "I'll reset myself. Suit, appear here as Astro Man." The room faded and with it, the pain. It reappeared and now he could see clearly. He hopped to his feet and examined the pile of unconscious bodies. "Comet Girl sure knows how to pack a punch."

Bridget giggled. Uncle George rubbed her head. "You can say that again."

Jeremy pulled the raygun from its holster and dialed in the gravity ray. He pointed it at the door and pulled the trigger. It burrowed into the metal. A red glow spread across the door as the beam dissolved the molecular cohesion, disintegrating a hole into the thick metal.

Blue Nova flashed to a stop in front of Jeremy. "About time. What took ya?"

Jeremy pointed at the pile of men. "Needed to clean up after ourselves."

Mickey smiled and slapped Jeremy on the shoulder. "Way to go, Bucko. That'll teach 'em."

"It wasn't me. Thank Comet Girl here. I was ready to surrender."

Mickey tussled her hair. "I should have known when I heard an explosion." He turned back to Jeremy. "But now what?"

"First, let's get out of here. No doubt they

have cameras all over this place. We can't discuss plans here. You take yours and Bridget's bodies. I'll take Uncle George's and my body in my ship. Comet Girl can fly. We'll meet again once we are clear of this place and figure out what to do."

Mickey nodded. "Sounds good. Let's do this."

Bridget gave a thumbs up. "Yes. Let's."

Uncle George said, "Anything to get out of here."

Mickey picked up his and Bridget's bodies, and Jeremy grabbed his own while Uncle George and Bridget followed him through the doorway. "Watch your step. The edges of the door are still hot."

Once into the hanger, Jeremy called out, "Suit, call ship." A dark jet-like aircraft materialized in the center of the hanger. The wings slicked back and pointed upwards at the tips. The rear tale marked the shape of a V. The glass hatch raised open from the back where the ship's nose narrowed to a point and angled slightly downward. Uncle George crawled into the back seat.

Jeremy settled his body into Uncle George's lap. "Sorry for the tight quarters, Uncle."

"Just get us out of here."

Jeremy saluted. "Sir, yes, sir." He hopped into the pilot's seat and lowered the hatch. After firing up the space jet, it rose from the ground. Jeremy aimed the ship's gravity ray and blasted the hanger doors. A red glow spread from the center followed by the disappearing wall. Sunlight poured in as the hole grew. Jeremy shoved the throttle forward. The ship accelerated toward the door and into the air of freedom.

Jeremy engaged the radio in his suit. "Mick, I'm going to send the government a Christmas present. Give me a minute."

"Gotcha."

Jeremy banked and came back around to the hanger door. He flipped the ship's camera on and filmed the smoke rising from the side of a mountain. As he dove back into the hanger, slowed to a stop, hovered around, and then blasted back out, he added the following audio narrative:

"Dear Mr. President and members of Congress, what you are seeing here is the secret base of a hidden military unit, or so I've been told. They kidnapped Astro Man, Blue Nova, and Comet Girl in order to steal our power. I was told you do not know of this unit, that it doesn't exist in the books. They threatened to ignore our constitutional rights upon capturing us. Even threatening to kill innocent civilians if we didn't cooperate. You can see the coordinates displayed on the video of the site's location. I'm sure you'll figure out how to proceed with this information. Thank you."

Jeremy saved the file, then addressed an email to the president, top cabinet members, and key members of congress, attached the video, and hit send. Jeremy couldn't help but grin. Even if some were in on the plot, now that it was exposed it would die a quick death. If it was truly a hidden organization, investigations and prosecutions were sure to follow.

Jeremy opened up the radio. "Blue Nova and Comet Girl. Operation Christmas Gift has been completed."

"What was the gift?" Mickey responded.

"The gift of truth. When truth is brought to light, it forces changes. Usually big changes." Jeremy smiled. "See that plateau I'm headed to?"

"Yes."

"We'll all met there. We can't return to our homes now. We'll have to take our bodies to Titan and figure out a plan of attack from there. We'll discuss the details on the plateau."

"Will do."

Jeremy focused as he angled the ship for a landing. Now he not only had lost his normal life because of these powers, he'd lost the last semblance of normalcy he had left: a home.

Uncle George placed a hand on his shoulder. "Jeremy, you've done good. I'm right proud of ya."

Jeremy smiled. He hadn't lost everything. He still had family and friends. And that mattered more than being normal. Now that was a real Christmas gift.

"Merry Christmas, Uncle. I love you too."

Chapter 1

Bridget pointed at one of the many monitors along one wall of the control room. "There he is! I knew it."

Jeremy glanced up. "Who?"

"The Grinch."

Jeremy focused on the screen she pointed at. "The Grinch?"

"Yeah, you know. Who stole Christmas?"

A man on the screen, dressed in an outfit that appeared to mimic the Grinch, slid open a window and climbed into the house. Ironically, it was Christmas Eve.

Bridget shook her head. "Last year, it was Santa. Now this."

"And you remember what happened last year?"

"Yes, it was a trap."

Jeremy stuffed the new superhero mask in his pocket and rose from his chair. "Would they be so stupid as to think we'd fall for it again, two years in a row?"

Jeremy sighed. "Problem is, if it isn't another trap, someone is going to have their Christmas stolen by a real grinch. If I go as Inviso Dude, I might be able to check before committing myself to it."

She shook her head. "That also means you'll be going solo. Too risky."

Jeremy nodded. "You're right." He'd done that too often before and ended up getting caught. Even as Inviso Dude. "I should take

Mickey with me. As Blue Nova, he can pretty much stay out of sight as well."

Bridget crossed her arms. "And what? I'm just supposed to stay here while you two get all the glory?"

Jeremy smiled. "Oh, why not come along too? Just stay hidden. We don't want to give ourselves away before we're ready."

Mickey's voice rang through the control room behind them. "Not going anywhere without me, are you?"

Jeremy spun around and smiled. "Just in time Mick. We have a situation similar to last year, except this time, Grinch instead of Santa."

Mickey frowned. "You're not thinking of going down there are you?"

"Yes, but we'll be more careful this time. I'm going as Inviso Dude, Bridget's staying hidden, and you'll hide as Blue Nova. We'll check it out before doing anything to reveal ourselves."

Mickey sighed. "I don't like it. Most Christmas Eve robberies we'd never know about anyway. Let's let this one be."

Jeremy put a hand on Mickey's shoulder. "Mick, it's not only because some kids might lose Christmas. If this is another trap, we need to find out who is doing it. I thought we'd shut down that special unit last year. If they are back in operation, they'll keep coming after us. Better to go into a trap knowingly than not being aware, don't you think?"

Mickey scratched his chin. "Bucko, you make some sense, for once. Let's go in."

Jeremy entered the coordinates into his suit. "Suit, appear at coordinates as Inviso Dude."

The cold steel of the space station on Titan vanished to be replaced by a wind whipping chills through the trees of a residential neighborhood. Bridget materialized as Comet Girl behind a tree, and Mickey as Blue Nova just out of sight.

Jeremy scanned the street. A news van recorded the event, just like last year. Over his communicator he said, "Mick, I'm going to see if anyone is hiding in the van. While I'm doing that, speed into the house and knock the burglar out. Don't bring him outside, just tie him up and make sure the presents he took are put back."

"You've got it."

Mickey disappeared in a blur. Jeremy worked his way toward the van, being as quiet as he could. He circled around the trees, staying out of sound range. The strong wind whistling through the trees helped mask any crackling leaves under his feet. He reached the side of the van and stuck his head through the metal.

Inside the van, two men sat at chairs bolted to the floor. Technical equipment surrounded them, complete with blinking lights and switches.

Camera and transmitting equipment? Nothing too suspicious here. Jeremy focused on the uniforms. Not US military, but they did look similar. Except patches on their side displayed in capital letters the acronym "ESEL." Who could that be? He didn't know any news stations with that call sign in the area.

One of the men turned to the other. "The Grinch is out. I repeat, the Grinch is out."

"Bucko," Mickey sounded over the com. "I've knocked him out and tied him up. Getting ready to put the presents back."

The other man in the van nodded. "Initiate Subspace."

Jeremy didn't like the sound of that. He pulled his head out of the van. "Mick, Bridget, return to base now! This is a trap."

"Rodger," Mickey responded.

"Got it," Bridget returned.

Jeremy started to speak the command, but grew lightheaded. The scenery wavered for a second before snapping back into place. Jeremy rubbed his head as he said, "Suit, appear as Astro Man."

The neighborhood vanished and then the control room materialized. Jeremy checked the monitor. A news piece ran on the recently elected president's plans once sworn in.

Mickey and Bridget appeared beside him. Mickey faced Jeremy. "Did you feel that phase in and out?"

"Yes. How about you, Bridget?"

She nodded. "Very strange feeling. But what was it?"

Jeremy shrugged. "I had my head in the van when they said the Grinch was down. Like they were monitoring him. Then they said something about initiating subspace. That's when I warned you both to return to base."

Bridget sat on a stool. "Well, they failed. They didn't get us this time."

"But what was that phased feeling?" Mickey asked.

Jeremy thought for a second. "If they initiated a subspace signal, it's possible it could have affected our virtual feed. We don't know they were trying to get us."

Mickey shoved a hand at the monitors. "Why else would someone fake a newscast? They know we monitor these feeds."

Jeremy turned on his heels and headed out the doors. "Better check on our bodies. I can't imagine they could do anything from here, but best to check."

They stepped down the virtual steel corridor, stopping before a door. It slid back and they entered the medical room. Their three bodies lay on the beds, IVs in as usual. The medical robot hummed over them, taking readings.

When the secret military unit captured their bodies last Christmas, they decided the only safe place to keep them was on Titan. It meant frequent trips to get real food and supplies, but it worked. Occasionally they would haul Uncle George and Natalie to the station for a visit.

But it meant any visits to Earth, short of flying their real bodies back to Earth, were by their virtual bodies. Going to school, even visiting Uncle George and Natalie.

Jeremy met Mickey and Bridget's eyes. "Let's return to our bodies for a bit. They probably need stretching anyway. We've been virtual for a while now."

Mickey nodded. "Good idea."

Jeremy pulled a mask out of his pocket and placed it on a counter.

Bridget scrunched her mouth. "What's that?"

"Don't tell, but it's Natalie's Christmas present."

Her eyes lit up. "Great, but what is it?"

Jeremy lifted it from the counter so that it dangled from his fingers. "A mask."

Mickey gasped. "Not like ours, is it?"

Jeremy nodded. "Holbreth gave it to me about a month ago. I've been saving it for a Christmas present for Natalie."

Mickey slapped his forehead. "Bucko! Just what I need! Having her around showing me up all the time." He pointed a finger at Jeremy. "You know how she feels about being virtual anyway. She probably won't like it."

Jeremy let it fall back to the counter. "I know. She may hate it. But I think she might be ready for it. She regrets not going with us when we leave."

Mickey laughed. "Bucko, that's just what

you want to think she's thinking. She gets a good night's sleep and wakes up to go with you to school and wherever else. I think she's perfectly happy."

"We'll see. It's only an hour till dawn. So let's get back into our real bodies for a while, eat some real food, and then we can go home for Christmas."

As they nodded, Jeremy said, "Exit suit." His view shifted from Astro Man standing in the room in front of his body to seeing out his own eyes again. He yawned as he heard Mickey and Bridget give the same command. He disconnected the IV from its port.

Jeremy rose from his bed and met Mickey's eyes. "Mick, do you feel stiff like you've been laying for three days?"

Mickey bent his leg. "Interestingly, no. I don't."

Bridget leaped off her bed. "I think this virtual air is doing our bodies some good."

Jeremy stood up. "You may be right, Sis. Let's go get some food." Jeremy led the way to the mess hall.

It would have felt weird attending Christmas with family as a virtual being, if it wasn't for the fact that the virtual reality was so real. It wouldn't have crossed Jeremy's mind save that he caught Uncle George staring at him every once in a while.

Uncle George had cut down a tree the old fashioned way. He'd decorated it with lights and tinsel. Jeremy gained the distinct impression that it had been a long time since Uncle George had a reason to really decorate for Christmas. Maybe because he felt sorry for their parents having died and wanted to make the holiday special.

"Here's yours, BJ." Bridget held out a wrapped package.

Jeremy grinned, recalling two Christmases ago when she tripped and fell, throwing his present into the air. The Mind Game helmet. In some ways, Jeremy wished it had broken on the floor that day. Maybe his parents would still be alive if it had.

He reached out for the gift. "Thanks you, Sis." He rattled it next to his ear. "I wonder what it could be?"

"Open it and find out already!"

Jeremy chuckled with the rest as he ripped the paper open. He pulled out a red and blue striped scarf. "Cool. I can use this on cold nights."

Everyone stared at him. Jeremy gulped. There were no cold nights on the space station. "Hey, virtual bodies need comfort too."

Natalie, dressed in a blue, short-sleeved blouse and jeans, grabbed a present under the tree and gave it to Jeremy. "Here, virtual man."

Jeremy smiled at her. She smiled back. He ripped the paper off and opened the box. He reached in and pulled out a watch. He nodded. "Sweet. Mine's a bit old."

"But it isn't just a watch. Mickey helped me work on it."

Uncle George chuckled. "If Mickey worked on it, no telling what it will do."

Natalie waved a hand at Uncle George. "Nothing that crazy. But if you push the button on the top right, it will give you a weather report on the screen. The bottom-right button taps into the virtual communication link, even when you aren't virtual. The bottom-left button initiates a homing beacon that registers on the virtual waves. For when you get captured by another alien—"

Bridget laughed and pointed at Jeremy. "Now that's a feature he needs."

Jeremy grinned. "It only happened three times."

"And . . ." Natalie lifted a finger. "The top-left button shifts the watch between watch mode and special ops mode."

Jeremy put the watch on his wrist. "I was going to ask how one set the time on this thing if none of the buttons could do it."

Jeremy reached under the tree and snagged a present for Uncle George. "Appears to be from Bridget, Uncle."

He accepted the wrapped box and gently removed the bow. "Now this is what I call a finely wrapped gift."

Bridget stuck her clasped hands between her legs and squeezed her shoulders tight, grinning as she watched him open it.

He slid the paper off the box and popped the top open. He dragged out a belt. He wrinkled his forehead and stared at Bridget.

"What?" Bridget's face fell.

Jeremy placed a hand on Bridget's shoulder. "Sis, Uncle wears suspenders and overalls. He doesn't use belts."

Bridget bowed her head. "I'm sorry. I didn't think about that."

Uncle George laughed and rubbed her hair. "Thank you, little angel. I've been thinking I should give belts a shot. I do, when called for, dress up." He stroked his beard.

Bridget raised her eyes to him. "When? I've never seen you dressed up."

"Well . . ." He coughed. "Wasn't going to say anything, but I do have a lady friend in town I've been wanting to visit. But without a belt, I wasn't sure she'd give me the time of day."

Bridget waved a hand at him. "Oh, Uncle. You can't expect me to believe that."

He pulled his head back and widened his eyes. "You don't think I have any romance in me?"

Natalie and Jeremy giggled under their breaths.

Bridget put her hands on her hips. "Uncle George. No silly. I meant I don't believe she would care that much about a belt." Bridget smiled. "But I'm glad you'll use it, anyway." She rose from her chair and pulled a present from under the tree. She read the tag, "From Jeremy to Natalie." She giggled as she handed the present to Natalie. "I know what it is, I know what it is!"

Natalie shook her head as she received the present and unwrapped it. She pulled the mask out of the box. She raised an eyebrow. "What is this?"

Jeremy grinned. "A mask."

Her eyes widened. "Oh, you mean like yours?"

Jeremy nodded.

She stared at it for a moment, her face blank. Without saying a word, she put the mask back in the box, placed it to the side, pulled another present out from the tree. "This one is for you, Little One. I'm going to get some coffee. Be right back." She rose and walked out.

Bridget held her gift in her hand. "What's wrong?"

Jeremy met Uncle George's gaze. Uncle George nodded to go after her. Jeremy jumped up and entered the kitchen. Natalie stood over the sink, her hands on the edge of the counter. She was bowing her head over the sink, breathing heavily.

Jeremy put a hand on her shoulder. "Sorry. I was hoping you might feel excited about it."

She turned to face him. Her wet eyes glistened in the morning sunlight. "Jeremy, how many times have you told me you wished this would have never happened to you? And now you want to drag me back into it too?"

"But you always look so sad when I leave to go fight crime without you."

She stared out the window. "I am. Yes. I want to be with you, but . . ."

Jeremy rubbed her back. "But you are still afraid of the virtual world."

She nodded. "I don't want to be controlled like that again."

"Holbreth designed this to be like ours. Only your voice can activate it or exit it. No one can break in and take you over like last time."

She returned her gaze to him. "Can you guarantee that? Is it impossible?"

Jeremy shrugged. "I don't think anything is 100% guaranteed. But this is about as close as you could expect to get to it."

Natalie blinked. "Nope. I can get 100% certainty by not putting it on."

Jeremy sighed. "Yes. Of course. I just thought . . . you'd want, I mean, I wanted . . ." Jeremy brought his lips to hers and savored a kiss. He parted from her soft lips and focused on her eyes. "I wanted you to be with me. I don't like having part of my life without you."

The corner of her lips turned up. "If I didn't know better, that sounded like a marriage proposal."

Jeremy pulled back. "Uh, no. Not meant to be. But . . ." He stomped his foot. "I do love you, and want you by my side as I fight crime." He placed a hand on her shoulder. "I was hoping you'd feel the same way."

Natalie leaned against the counter. Her brown, shoulder-length hair created a halo in the sunlight. "I do feel the same way. But this fear inside of me is hard to ignore. Despite your assurances, I don't feel safe."

Jeremy breathed deeply. "I understand. Give it some thought, at least. Then if you still feel the same way after a couple days, I'll get you a different present."

She cracked a smile. "Okay." Then reached out and swallowed Jeremy into her arms. "Thank you for understanding."

Jeremy hugged her back. "What are true friends for?" He released her and held her hand. Come on, let's go back to the party."

She nodded and followed him back into the room.

Chapter 2

The details of the control room shifted into focus from the black void as Jeremy appeared. Mickey sat at the monitors. The one he viewed displayed text instead of a video feed.

Jeremy said, "Hey Mick, what are you doing?"

He jerked his head up from the screen. "Oh, not much. Just looking through my list of superheros. Wanting to find something new to try."

"Find anything yet?"

"Nothing that hit my cool meter."

Jeremy sat next to him. "So, how was your Christmas?"

He nodded. "Pretty good. Liked your gift."

Jeremy shook his head. "Not nearly as cool as the one you helped Natalie with." Jeremy glanced around. "Where's Bridget?"

Mickey shrugged. "She's your sister, not mine."

Bridget said, "I'm right here."

Jeremy scanned the room. "I don't see you."

"That's because I'm using Holbreth's Christmas present. A new superhero. Inviso Girl."

Jeremy smiled. "Like my Inviso Dude. We can be invisible together. Hey, maybe I can see you while I'm invisible. Let me try."

Jeremy stood. "Suit, appear as Inviso Dude."

The room went black and then returned. It appeared the same as before, except now in the middle of the room stood a ghostly form of his sister.

Bridget giggled. "I see you!"

"And I see you, Sis."

Mickey chuckled. "Now that your both invisible, I can rule the world!"

Jeremy grinned. "Suit, appear here as myself."

After returning to normal, he sat down at the screen. "So, Sis. You say Holbreth gave us new superheros for Christmas?"

"Yeah. He told me about it yesterday."

Jeremy jerked around. "What? You talked with him yesterday? When?"

She said, "Suit, appear here as myself." She materialized wearing jeans and a shirt. Her blonde hair dangled over her forehead. "Yeah. You may recall I took a nap yesterday afternoon."

Mickey shook his head. "Little One, you are getting too devious. But certainly you didn't plan on meeting Holbreth."

"No, he just showed up. When he told me of his Christmas presents, I asked him not to tell you guys. So he left a message with me."

Jeremy glanced at Mickey. "What message?"

Bridget cleared her throat. "He said there was a disturbance in the force." She shrugged. "He said you'd know what that meant."

Mickey scratched his head. "It's a line from an old movie. Usually used when someone died or something had gone terribly wrong. But it isn't like Holbreth to use such cryptic lines."

Jeremy held a finger up. "Unless he thought someone might be listening in."

"But he wasn't going over communicators. He was here in person."

Jeremy shook his head. "Mick, keep in mind, he was here in person, but virtually. The 'force' had to be a reference to the virtual world. He may have feared someone could listen in on our talking."

"Well then, we've just given it away. How else are we going to discuss this?"

Bridget laughed. "In our real bodies, of course."

Jeremy hit his forehead with his palm. "Duh! Exit suit." He heard the others say it as the control room disappeared to be replaced by the sick bay. He blinked his eyes, disconnected his IV, and pulled himself off the bed as Mickey and Bridget did the same. Jeremy stretched and flexed his arms. He was overdue for some exercise. He'd been virtual too long.

"Okay, Sis, did Holbreth say anything else? Did he explain what he meant?"

She sat on the edge of the bed. "I asked, since I had no idea what he meant. He only said you'd know what he was talking about, and he didn't know enough to say anything more."

Mickey hopped off the bed. "Apparently he's noticed some oddities in the virtual world and wanted us to keep our radar active." He headed for the door. "Let's get something to eat while we talk. I'm hungry."

They nodded in agreement and followed him. Jeremy pulled up beside him as they stepped down the hall. "Oddities like that phase in and out we felt last night at that robbery."

Mickey nodded. "That would certainly qualify."

"Question is, what happened? I've not felt differently. We weren't trapped like last time. I'm not sure what it might have done."

Bridget tugged on his pants leg as they entered the mess hall. "Maybe it did something to the virtual energy if Holbreth is worried about that."

Mickey stared at Bridget, and then Jeremy.

"Little One may be on to something. But the hard question is what could it have done?"

Jeremy shook his head. "And who are they? What does ESEL stand for?"

They grabbed some sandwiches and chips, and headed for the control room. Once in, mouths munched on food as Jeremy and Mickey sat at the monitors and started checking their list of superheros.

Jeremy pointed at the screen. "Look, right there is something new. It says, 'Latest changes.'" Jeremy touched the link on the screen. A superhero name popped up.

Mickey stared at his screen. "Mine says Chameleon Soldier and Captain Subspace."

Jeremy's eyes widened. "Subspace?" He turned to face Mickey. "That was the code name for whatever it was that the man initiated when you were taking down the Grinch robber."

Mickey continued staring at his screen. "You think this might have been added when that phase hit?"

Jeremy sat back in his chair. "Too much of a coincidence, wouldn't you say? They would have no clue I heard the name of their program. I'd say this has to be it."

Mickey nodded his head toward Jeremy's screen. "What about you? Anything suspicious?"

Jeremy checked. "Just one entry. Magic Man." Jeremy spun around to face Bridget. "What about you, Sis? Did you have more than one new superhero?"

She shook her head. "Nope."

Jeremy pointed at Mickey's screen. "See what the description for Captain Subspace is. Maybe that will give us a clue."

Mickey touched the description link. "Says Captain Subspace can warp to another location in seconds, and has rays that disrupt reality at the sub-atomic level."

Jeremy rubbed his chin. "Nothing definitive. But this does worry me on a different level. Someone has the ability to insert an add-on program into the virtual world. It's probably a virus. Once activated, who knows what it might do."

Bridget tapped Jeremy on the shoulder. "Doesn't this fall into an oddity? Shouldn't we tell Holbreth?"

Jeremy stood up. "Yes, I think we should. Why don't you two use an Eagle to return to Earth in the flesh and get some supplies from Uncle George. Meanwhile, I'll head to Zori, and relay this info to Holbreth in person, and see what all he has to say."

Mickey nodded. "Sounds like a plan."

Bridget put her hands on her hips. "Why can't I go?"

A voice in the back of the control room said, "Because I want to go."

Jeremy caught his breath and slowly turned around. Natalie stood in the control room wearing shorts and a loose blouse. She'd pulled her hair back into a ponytail. She walked briskly toward Jeremy.

Jeremy smiled. "You came."

She smiled weakly. "I couldn't sleep. Felt lonely. Decided why not? Let's give this a try."

"But I never had the chance to tell you how to do it."

Bridget bounced toward Natalie and wrapped her in a hug. "I told her how to operate it. Another reason I didn't come right away." She finished her squeeze and stood back. "I'm so glad I'm not going to be the only girl here."

Mickey saluted her. "Welcome aboard."

She smiled back at him. "So, you're going to Zori."

Jeremy shuffled his feet. "Yes. Are you sure you're ready for that? Maybe you should take some time to feel comfortable before facing Zori again. Bridget could go with me. I don't want you to have flashbacks or anything."

Her lips tightened. "Look. I'm here be- cause . . ." She glanced at Mickey. "Because I decided to face my fears. What better place to face my fears than Zori?"

"If you're sure."

Natalie relaxed. "Yes. I'm sure."

Jeremy nodded. "Sis, reacquaint Natalie with the station. I've got a few more things to tie up with Mickey before we leave."

Bridget started to move. Natalie pointed a finger at Jeremy. "I've been here before. You aren't trying to leave without me, are you?"

"Don't worry. I won't. Since we are keeping our bodies here, though, you need to know a few more things about the station."

Natalie stared a moment into Jeremy's eyes, then left the room holding Bridget's hand.

Mickey stood next to Jeremy. "I guess I was right about how she might feel. But you won in the end. She's here."

"Yes, and that's what worries me. Some- thing isn't right with her."

Mickey laughed. "Now there's a switch. I've always been the suspicious one when it came to her."

"That's just it, Mick. You were right about how she'd react to the mask. She nearly had a meltdown when she opened the box and pulled out the mask. You should have seen the fear in her eyes. How does she go from that, to stand- ing confidently before us, ready to go to Zori where she experienced the takeover of her vir- tual body?"

Mickey shrugged. "I've always taken her to have a strong nature. Maybe it's just as she said? She's facing her fears. After all, that phase thing couldn't have anything to do with her virtually. One, Holbreth created her mask well before the phase event happened. Two, she wasn't there virtually at the time. Whatever all they did, they needed us in the vicinity to introduce that program into our virtual systems. I doubt it affected her mask that had never been activated until tonight."

Jeremy breathed deep. "You're probably right, but there is another issue if this really is Natalie. Up until tonight, we've had no questions about the stability of the virtual world. We're taking a risk not telling her the danger has increased. She could end up being taken over. Maybe already has simply by putting on the mask." Jeremy rubbed his forehead. "She's going to kill me if that is true."

Mickey slapped Jeremy on the back. "Bucko, if it will help, I'll check on her body when I'm at your Uncle George's for supplies. Make sure she actually put on this mask. It may not tell us if her virtual body was taken over, but it will tell us if that is indeed her and not some new program introduced into the system."

"True. We don't know if the new superhero for you is the only thing that subspace routine changed. Of course, if this isn't Natalie, or she's been taken over again, I could be leading whoever it is right into Zori. Can we take that chance?"

Mickey stared at the floor for a few seconds. "Too many unknowns. If it were up to me, she'd stay here."

Jeremy nodded. "Definitely too many unknowns. Which means we don't want to alert her that we are suspicious, if it is whoever is behind all this. Which means I can't have her in the meeting with Holbreth, or tell her why she can't come. Any ideas on how to convey that? She seems dead set on going to Zori."

"Now that you mention it, it's strange how bad she wants to go to Zori. Maybe tell her you don't love her anymore and don't want her around."

Jeremy jerked his head around to face Mickey. "What? I can't do that. What if this is the real Natalie? What if in revenge she becomes our sworn enemy?"

Mickey smiled. "Bucko! You forget? The making up part is always the best."

Jeremy threw up his hands. "Ah, great relationship advice from someone who's never had one."

"Did so." Mickey grinned. "In third grade. Her name was Amanda."

Jeremy chuckled. "What did you do? Kiss her once?"

Mickey lost his smile. "How did you know?"

Jeremy patted Mickey on the back. "Back to now. I still need—"

"Are we ready, yet?" Natalie and Bridget entered the control room.

Jeremy scratched behind his head. "Ah, Natalie. We've run into a snag. We need to run some diagnostics on your software to make sure it's working as expected. Now's not a good time—"

"You're ditching me? After all the effort and struggle I went through to be here for you?"

Jeremy shook his head. "No, not ditching you. But we'll have to take a rain check. You see, it's just too risky for you to go all the way to Zori without test-driving your virtual self for a while. You need time to make sure everything is working—"

"I'm here aren't I? I don't feel anything bad other than what you're saying. I came to be with you. I didn't come here to watch you disappear for three days."

Jeremy ran his fingers through his hair. "I'm sorry. But its been this long. Surely you can wait for a while longer. Mickey can help you get used to the virtual experience while I'm gone. When I get back, we'll spend plenty of time together. But it is too risky this—"

"I'm taking the risk. Not you. You're just scared to let me into your world."

"I'm not! Why would I have given you the mask to begin with?"

"Exactly! Why? When I finally overcome my fear and become virtual, now you want to ignore that and go do your own thing without me?"

Jeremy bowed his head. "I can't bring you with me this time. I may be able to explain later. You'll have to trust me on this one. It's probably best if you exit your suit now."

Natalie gritted her teeth and clenched her fists into tight balls. She released a half scream, half grunt, and then said, "Exit suit." She vanished.

Jeremy collapsed into a chair. He could feel his eyes watering.

Bridget put a hand on Jeremy's arm. "What was that all about? Why did you ditch Natalie?"

"I'll tell you on the way to Zori. Looks like you're coming with me." Jeremy wiped his eyes with his sleeves. "Mick, check on her. Comfort her if she needs it. Try to make her understand I still love her."

Mickey patted Jeremy's shoulder. "You've got it, Bucko. At least this way I should be able to find out if she was controlled by anyone, as long as I can see her mask with no one attached to it."

Jeremy breathed deep. "Thanks." He stood and held Bridget's hand. "Let's go, Sis. Suit, appear at the Zori space station as myself."

The control room vanished, but the knot in his gut didn't.

Chapter 3

Mickey landed the Eagle ship on Uncle George's plateau located on a mountain in Montana. He kept the ship cloaked in case ESEL was watching. Best to not be seen walking to the house as well.

"Suit, appear here as Blue Nova." The control cabin of the ship vanished and then reappeared. Mickey checked his hands to make sure he'd changed. He opened the hatch and zipped across the field. The cold, mountain night air chilled him even at super-speed. Snow dotted the ground. The only evidence of his presence was the swish of knee-high grass as he blazed past it.

He sped into Uncle George's living room. Night lights flickered in the hallway, but otherwise, all was dark. He carefully stepped his way down the hall and stopped at Natalie's door. Her light was on. He breathed deep and then lightly knocked. "Natalie, it's me, Mick. I wanted to check on you."

He heard footsteps shuffling around for a moment, then silence. He started to knock again when the door cracked open.

Natalie's red eyes were offset by lips pressed firmly together, daring him to say anything wrong. "You mean, someone actually cares?"

Mickey paused. He wasn't good at these kinds of personal interactions. "Can I come in? I just want to talk for a moment."

She stared into his eyes for five seconds before opening the door and heading back to sit on her bed. She glanced at Mickey but averted her eyes as if she might hide the fact she'd been crying. "Well, what do you want to talk about? The weather?"

Mickey smiled. "I see your sarcastic bent didn't die with that Zorian."

She cracked a bare smile before it faded away. "Why did Jeremy not want me along?"

"I'll tell you the full truth if you show me the mask."

She met his eyes. "What? Why?"

"Just show me the mask. I'll fill you in on everything once I've seen that."

She huffed and pointed to the trash can. "It's in there."

Mickey grimaced. "You threw it away?"

She gritted her teeth. "After what he did? Yes I threw it away! I don't want anything to do with the virtual world. And I'm done with him too."

Mickey fished the mask out of the can. "You might want to hold that thought until after I've told you the whole story." He examined the mask. It certainly did appear to be her virtual mask. But what if this was a virtual copy of the mask? "But one other thing I need you to do."

She threw up her hands. "Come on! I showed you the mask."

"Say aloud, 'Exit' you know what."

"Seriously?" She stared at Mickey for a moment, then growled out, "Exit suit." She remained on the bed, staring at Mickey. "Satisfied?"

Mickey nodded. "Sorry, but had to make sure you were not virtual before I related this info. Had to make sure your virtual body had not been taken over."

Her mouth dropped open. "But Jeremy assured me just yesterday morning that the chance of that happening again was near zero. Why the sudden concern?"

Mickey sat on the bed next to her. "We just discovered the problem right before you arrived. It appears someone has successfully inserted a new superhero program into my options, and we suspect it's from an organization we only know the acronym for, ESEL. We aren't sure what else they've been able to accomplish. So when you arrived, all eager to go to Zori when before you feared even becoming virtual, we feared the worst, that you had put on the mask and been taken over by ESEL with the intent to gain control of the virtual machine and programming."

She bowed her head. "Couldn't he have checked me out like you're doing now before he left?"

Mickey bobbed his head. "Maybe. But we didn't have enough time to figure out the best way to do it. Since Jeremy was going to Holbreth to speak to him about this issue, we couldn't take the chance to bring you along. I think you caught him off guard."

She stared at the floor for a few seconds. "Well, you can tell him I wasn't being controlled by anyone, and I really was ready to go to Zori." She sucked in a deep breath. "Does he have any idea how hard it was for me to put on that mask and be there?" She heaved and rubbed her eyes with her right hand. "I sacrificed my security to be with him, and he tossed it away like it was nothing."

Mickey patted her back. "He does love you. He asked me to make sure you knew that."

"Actions speak louder than words."

"But I told you why he did it."

"I was so scared." She struggled to not burst out crying.

"You could have fooled me." Mickey moved his hand to her opposite shoulder and gave her a hug. He was hugging his best friend's girl. *Awkward!* But Jeremy did tell him to comfort her, and this felt like the right way to do that.

Natalie let out a groaning cry and wrapped her arms around Mickey's neck, crying on his shoulder.

Mickey held her tightly in an effort to comfort her. He didn't know what to say as she continued to bawl. His shoulder grew wet. He rubbed his hand along her back and neck; she started regaining control. He continued the action. She calmed down and hugged him tighter. The uncomfortable feeling grew again, not only because she was still hugging him, but because a flash of pleasant energy rolled through him. He stopped rubbing her back, released her, and stared at the walls.

Natalie rubbed his back in return and pulled away. "Sorry. I know I'm acting like some love-struck girl, crying and all."

"You had good reason. Like you said, it wasn't easy for you to face your fear like that, as bravely as you were doing."

She smiled. "Thank you. I'm glad someone gets it." She pulled a tissue from a box and wiped her eyes.

Mickey smiled awkwardly. On one hand, he had successfully helped her. She'd actually complimented him. After all the fights and suspicions they'd had for each other, all the challenges, all the antagonistic sparring, now she had showed him appreciation. That was a first.

Mickey stood up. He needed to gain some distance from her to counter his feelings. Maybe this would change the dynamic. "So, are you still ready to face those fears again?" He held out the mask.

She stared at it. "But what about the fear of me being taken over?"

"I doubt you're susceptible. We suspect our

presence at a location where they initiated a program they called 'subspace' tapped into our virtual feeds somehow to add in the program. If anyone was going to be taken over, it'd probably be me, and I haven't been. You weren't even there, and your mask was created well before that happened."

She stood. "So there is still little to no chance I'll be taken over by someone?"

"To be truthful, I don't know what the chance of it is. But based on what I know right now, I'd say not a very big chance."

She bit her lip. "Shouldn't I wait until Jeremy gets back?"

He shrugged. "You can if you want, but if I were you, I'd want to get acquainted with your superheroes and be ready to roll by the time Jeremy returns. Plus . . ." Mickey grinned. "It will be boring at the station by myself. I'd appreciate the company. Who knows, once you get a feel for things, we could go on some missions together."

She nodded. "That makes sense. And I would hate for you to be all alone for the next three days." She accepted the mask and slid it on.

Mickey threw out a hand. "Hold on. You'll want to lay down first."

Her eyes grew big. "Oh! Of course." She lay on the bed and closed her eyes. "Suit, appear here as myself." A duplicate Natalie materialized, standing by her bed. Her confident eyes had returned, no longer red with crying.

She breathed deeply as she stared at her body lying on the bed. "This is an odd feeling."

"Tell me about it. You have no idea until you've saved your own body from a burning building."

She grabbed his hand. "Really, though, I want to thank you for helping me through this."

She pulled him to her and kissed his lips. Her soft skin held his for a second before breaking away. Mickey stopped breathing and stared at Natalie's eyes. The excitement coursing through him demanded he kiss her back, but he knew he couldn't. He sucked in air and let it out slowly.

Natalie stared at the floor. "I . . . uh, what were we going to do now?"

Mickey spoke, but it sounded weak, as if breathless. "Get supplies and fly them back to Titan." Mickey started to head for the door.

Natalie's hand grabbed his shoulder. "Mickey, don't tell Jeremy about that. He may get the wrong idea, that it was more than just a thank you kiss."

Mickey cleared his throat. "I can see where he might think that."

"Are you okay? Your face is flushed."

How do you tell a woman she just gave you your first kiss, and it sent you into orbit? "I'll be fine. I wasn't expecting it is all."

"Sorry if it made you uncomfortable. But that is how I felt. The kiss came from the heart. There's nothing wrong with expressing thankfulness."

Mickey nodded. "Of course not. Just an I'm-thankful kiss. Understood. Now, let's collect those supplies and get them to Titan. This way." Mickey refrained from zipping out the door at super speed, though at the moment, he certainly wanted to. Instead, he walked out in a hurried pace.

———

The transporter room emerged from the darkness. A bald-headed Zorian, as they all were, manned the transporter controls. He smiled. "Been a while, though I never know what you're going to look like when you do come. Holbreth I assume?"

Jeremy hopped off the pad with Bridget following behind. "Yes. You remembered us?"

He nodded. "Go on ahead, I think you know the way. I'll let him know you're coming."

"Thanks."

Bridget waved. "Good to meet you." Bridget caught up to Jeremy as he worked his way down the steel hall. "How long has it been since you've been here?"

"About a year and a half."

"And he remembered who you were?"

Jeremy rubbed his chin. "You may have something there. More than you realize. The last time I was here not wearing a mask was almost two years ago, when I left the Mind Game. That said, I was a hero for taking out Rillian. Likely they know what I look like."

"I took out Rillian."

Jeremy patted her on the back. "Yes, you did. And kept Rillian from taking me out too."

They stopped at Holbreth's office and pressed the buzzer. The vid screen came to life with Holbreth's face.

He glanced to the side. "Hold on, I'll let you in. You'll find there are some, ah, extra security precautions since the last time you were here."

Jeremy met Bridget's eyes for a moment as the door slid open, revealing a short hallway. They stepped into it and the door shut behind them. A humming noise emanated around them for five seconds, and then the opposite door slid open. The pair entered Holbreth's office.

Jeremy pointed at the hallway jutting into the office. "Why the extra security?"

Holbreth pointed at chairs before his desk. "I'm glad you've come. We can talk freely in here. The extra security is to filter for viruses in your virtual feed, to make sure no one can eavesdrop on us or gain access to the programming controls in this room."

Jeremy settled into a seat. "So you suspect someone is attempting to introduce viruses into the virtual world too?"

Holbreth raised an eyebrow. "I take it you have seen some disturbances in the force as well?"

Bridget snickered as she sat down. "I'll say."

Jeremy leaned forward. "When you added new superheroes to our lists for Christmas, how many did you give each of us?"

"One each."

"Mickey had two new ones in his list. The virus was called Subspace."

Holbreth's brow wrinkled his bald head. He spun his chair around to a console and opened windows, entering commands. The list of Mickey's superheroes cascaded up the screen. He paused the list with his finger, and scrolled back up. He touched the name, and a window of code opened. A red flashing light at the bottom signaled foreign code.

He met Jeremy's eyes. "Most certainly a virus. How did you know? I'm assuming Mickey hasn't used it."

Jeremy proceeded to tell him what happened with the van, the phase shift, and how they'd discovered the new superhero in Mickey's list with the same name that the men referred to in the van.

Holbreth sat back in his chair, rubbing his forehead. "Very worrisome. So someone on Earth introduced a virus program into the virtual world's program here on Zori. That can only mean one thing."

"What?" asked Bridget.

"That the changes to the world I've noticed are not being introduced by anyone here on Zori, but by someone on your world. The only way they could do that is by piggybacking onto the virtual feeds created by your mask."

Jeremy shook his head. "Don't forget, we are not the only virtual items in our solar system. The whole Titan space station is virtual."

Holbreth snapped his fingers. "Of course. The feed for the station would be less noticeable. They use your feed to get from Earth to Titan, and then the station's feed to reach Zori."

"So, you've noticed other changes?"

Holbreth nodded. "Minor ones. Appeared to be tests. One changed the color of some houses on Zori. Another rounded the tips of the Raven space ships. I feared someone on Zori was hacking into the system like Rillian did, even though we've installed some safeguards to keep that from happening."

Holbreth returned to his screen. "One thing's for sure. We can't let this virus remain." He entered a command and the code in the window disappeared. He saved it, and overwrote the previous program as an empty file.

Jeremy sighed. "It looks like we'll have to lay low on the superhero front to avoid giving them any more opportunities to introduce anything else. Our next mission will be to find out who is doing this and stop them."

Bridget sat up. "Have you discussed any of this with the Overlords?"

Holbreth raised an eyebrow. "No, I have not. I was still trying to locate the source of these changes, and feared it might be them. I didn't want to alert them that I was onto them if they were responsible."

Jeremy knew the Overlords could have done that a long time ago if they wanted, but figured they wouldn't appreciate him telling the Zorians that. "Mind if Bridget and I check with them and see what they know about this?"

Holbreth waved his hand. "Be my guest. Let me know what you find out."

Bridget stood. "Can we eat here first? I'm not in the mood for seaweed salad."

Holbreth smiled. "Sure. Let's go eat lunch together before you leave."

Chapter 4

"See, this isn't so bad." Mickey waved his hand around the control room of the station on Titan. He sat before a terminal and touched an icon. He typed "Natalie" in a window, and a list of her superheroes scrolled up.

He hopped out of the chair and waved his palm toward the chair. "Here's the list of superheroes available to you. I'd recommend starting out with one or two of them. Best to get familiar with them slowly."

Natalie seated herself and studied the screen. "So, how many of your superheroes have you tried?"

Mickey thought for a couple of seconds and then laughed. "I guess three."

She smirked. "I thought you were more adventurous than that."

He shrugged. "Guess you get comfortable with a small number, and you don't go looking for more. But I probably should try out some others." He sat at a terminal next to hers. "I suppose I should try out Holbreth's Christmas present. Chameleon Soldier." He tapped on the screen a few times. "There it is. A master at weapons, carries a duel gun and rocket launcher, and an unending supply of explosives. He can blend in with any background to be invisible to those around him. He can glide with wings, and has a built in mini-grappling hook to scale walls and buildings up to twenty-five stories high."

She glanced at him. "Can he fly?"

"Uh . . ., no."

"Bummer." Natalie's eyes lit up. "This one sounds interesting. Starlight." She tapped the screen. "Says she can fly, even through space, at the speed of light. That's cool! And she can use the starlight to blind people, use it as an energy ray, force field, and to heal people."

"Sounds cool. Why don't you give that one a try?"

She nodded, stood, and then moved to the center of the room. "Appear here as Starlight."

She vanished for a second, and then a woman reappeared. A formfitting, silver one-piece covered her body. Silver-blue briefs, gloves, boots, cape, and a half-mask that allowed her hair to flow from the top, finished the outfit.

Mickey sat stunned. If he didn't know better, he'd think she was a model walking a runway.

As if she heard his thoughts, she swung around, swirling the cape through the air, giving him a full display. She lifted her hands up. "What do you think?"

Mickey realized his mouth hung open. He cleared his throat and glanced at the floor. Heat flooded his face. "Absolutely gorgeous."

She laughed. "Those astronaut outfits in Mind Game didn't do my figure any favors, I know."

He smiled. "That's the understatement of the year." He realized he was staring again. He spun himself around. "We should locate something simple for you to try out your powers." He scanned the monitors.

"That would be cool." She stepped beside him.

Her hand rested on his right shoulder. The contact acted like a beacon in the night. The more he tried not to think about it, the more he did. *I need to find something fast. Any-*

thing. He landed on a monitor. "There." He pointed.

A monitor showed a live newscast of a house fire. "See those coordinates? You enter them into your suit. For example, 'Suit, enter coordinates,' and then list them out as you see them on the screen. Or you can say, 'Suit, appear at coordinates,' list them out, '. . . as,' and say the hero you want to be. Got it?"

She nodded. She entered the coordinates. "Suit, appear at coordinates as Starlight." She vanished.

Mickey smiled, but it faded quickly. He wanted to be with her, but she was Jeremy's girl. He couldn't have feelings like this for her. But he did. He had to bury it. Not let them out. The last thing he wanted to do was let a girl come between them.

Mickey needed to follow her. Which hero would match hers and be useful for a house fire? He stood after entering the coordinates. "Suit, appear at coordinates as G Man."

A city block in China gelled into view. Fire units blasted water onto the house fire, roaring into the sky with a black cloud of smoke. Natalie stood directly in front of him, apparently trying to decide what to do.

Mickey stepped up behind her and placed a hand on her shoulder. She swung around. Mickey glanced toward the fire and yanked his hand off her. He didn't mean to encourage her advances. "What in your list of powers can put out a house fire or check the house for anyone trapped?"

She said, "I'm not sure."

"You often won't have time to check your list and think about it. Someone could be dying in there. What are you going to do?"

She stomped the ground. "I don't know! I only looked at the list once. Why don't you stop it?"

He nodded. "I could, but it is better if you get acquainted with your powers. I recall you can produce a shield with your starlight power."

Her eyes lit up. "I could use it to go into the fire and check for survivors."

"And . . . ?"

She shrugged.

"You can extend your field over the whole fire and suffocate it. Put a secondary shield around yourself so you don't lose all your air."

She smiled at him. "You're good at this."

Heat rose to his face again. "Get going. Remember, the worst that can happen is you die and return to your body. If you get stuck, let me know, then exit your suit."

She nodded and sucked in a deep breath. "Here I go." She jumped into the air and flew in a blur through the door of the house.

Mickey heard crashing and breaking wood. He almost started to run in after her, but held back. She needed to do this on her own. In a minute, a silver, shimmering dome rose over the house. The fire shrank until only glowing embers remained. The firefighters shut off their hoses since the water had been bouncing off the shield and falling to the ground.

The silver dome disappeared and then Starlight flew from the house. She tried to stop before Mickey, but she skidded, then tripped and fell into a bush.

"Mickey!" Natalie yelled out.

"Shush!" Mickey waved a hand at her. "No yelling out our real names in public. I'm G Man."

"Fine, G Man. Mind helping me out of here?"

He reached out a hand. "You're starting to sound more like your old self." She latched on and he pulled her out of the bush.

She kept a grip on his hand. "I feel so clumsy."

Mickey pointed at the house. "But you did put out the fire. Good job." The firefighters scurried around the partially charred house, rummaging through the rubble.

Natalie smiled. "So I did. Let's do more."

Mickey pulled his hand from hers. "Suit, appear as myself." China dimmed into darkness and the control room emerged. Natalie appeared next to him still suited up as Starlight.

She dropped back to the monitor listing her superheroes. "I saw another one that sounded interesting." She tapped a link and read for a moment. Then stood back. "Suit, appear here as Black Hole."

She vanished then reappeared. Mickey fell back into his seat. Before him stood a woman in black boots and gloves, black briefs, a black halter top, and a diamond-shaped eye-mask to match.

She spun around again. "Pretty cool, huh?"

He stared at her. "I'd say anyone would be pretty cool in that outfit. A lot of exposed skin there."

She patted her bare stomach. "It is a little sparse in the material department. But it covers all the necessary areas, don't you think?"

Mickey breathed deep. The suit left little to the imagination. "Uh . . . yeah. Sure." Of course, it covered more than a lot of two-piece bathing suits he'd seen. Still, for some reason, this had his heart racing. She must know. He couldn't hide it.

She drew close to him, took his hands, and lifted him to his feet. "Mickey, I think we need to be honest with each other. I—"

He placed a hand over her mouth. Her soft lips pressed against his palm. His blood pulsed in his neck. Everything said to kiss her. She obviously wanted it. He wanted it. Still . . . "I can't do this to Jeremy. We really need to keep this a working relationship."

She pulled back and stared at the floor. "I do love Jeremy, but I'm realizing it is more as a brother than a boyfriend." She met Mickey's eyes. "I don't feel the same way about him that I'm feeling about you right now."

"But he'll be devastated. I know him."

"Look, I never told him we were dating or going steady. I'm free to chose who I want to be with and date. Jeremy has nothing to do with this."

"But you kissed him, lots of times."

Natalie stared into his eyes. "Yes. I thought I was in love. And I do love him. He's kind, compassionate, smart, and—"

"Loyal to a fault." Confidence flowed back into him. "Loyal to me, to you. He'll take this as a betrayal. Maybe you don't feel you love him that deeply, but I know he loves you that much."

She sighed. "My relationship to Jeremy is between me and Jeremy. I'll deal with him. But what I'm talking about isn't me and Jeremy, but me and you. I can see you want me. Why can't I chose who I want to be with?"

Mickey opened his mouth but no words came out. Who was he to say who she should be with? Jeremy would be hurt, but there was nothing he could do to stop that if she really felt this way. And the thought of having some-one who wanted him as a boyfriend, who wanted to spend time with him, sparked like fireworks through his mind and body. She de-sired him!

Mickey grabbed her head and pulled it to his. He stopped millimeters from her lips. "So, are you saying you love me? That you want to be my girlfriend?"

Her eyes darted back and forth over his face. She pushed forward and connected with his lips. Her tongue danced around his for a few seconds; Mickey's heart bonded to hers as an excitement filled its every beat.

She released him. "Does that answer your question?"

He responded with his own kiss, treasuring the experience. A tearing sensation grew where her hands met his skin. His back, as if a powerful vacuum cleaner ripped him apart, disintegrated atom by atom. The irresistible pull compressed him into a single stream flowing into her hands.

The control room disappeared and the medical bay focused into view through half-open eyes. He shook his head. She must have killed him somehow. He disconnected his IV and sat up to get his bearings.

Natalie, still dressed as Black Hole, jumped into the room and skidded to a halt. "I'm so sorry. I wasn't paying attention in the moment and I must have sucked you into a black hole."

Mickey shook his head. Sucked into a black hole. That described what he'd experienced with his desires. "No worries. That isn't the first time I've died virtually, and probably won't be the last. But being this is my real body, I'd prefer if you became yourself before any more kissy, kissy happens. I'm all out of real bodies to use."

She smiled. "Suit, appear here as myself." She disappeared and then reappeared in the shorts and t-shirt she arrived in.

Mickey couldn't believe how different he felt about her now. As she wrapped her arms around his neck, he sank into her embrace and kiss. A spark of life activated feelings he didn't known existed.

―――――

Jeremy and Bridget sloshed into the water lapping the edge of the lake. The blue sky of

Zori, dotted with orange-tinted clouds from the setting sun, cast is canopy over the lake and hills. The sunlight sparkled off the gentle waves, giving the lake an unnatural appearance.

Jeremy stopped as the water reached his knees. "This should be far enough." Jeremy recalled the first time he and Mickey found this lake and waded in. They thought monsters were attacking them at the time. The thoughts made him smile.

Bridget met Jeremy's eyes. "How long?"

"Don't know. Maybe someone forgot to turn it on. No one is expecting us."

Bubbles started rising to the surface of the water in two locations. Two long tubes reared into the air like giant snakes, then plunged over their bodies, sucking them into its "mouth."

Jeremy smiled as he splashed along the water tube. It spun around and through some curves, before throwing him into a shallow pond inside the underwater building. As Jeremy sloshed out of the water, Bridget splashed into another next to his and staggered out.

A big grin graced her face. "I wish I could live here."

"That could be arranged," a voice echoed.

Jeremy turned to find Jornash waiting for them by the door. "Jornash!"

Bridget ran and wrapped her arms around his scaly waist. "It's so good to see you again."

Jornash smiled as only a mereperson could. "And I, you, brave one. It has been many tides since we were together." His smile disappeared. "However, you rarely come to make social calls. What troubles you this time?"

Jeremy nodded. "Might be best if we discussed this in the control room for the virtual machine. My guess is you'll want to look at code."

"I thought as much." He waved them his way as he turned and went through the door. "We have noticed some intrusions into the virtual world. We're still trying to determine where they are from, but we've narrowed it down to Earth."

Jeremy pulled Bridget from staring out the transparent walls of the hallway as fish swam by. "So, you know it comes from Earth?"

Jornash turned down another hall. "Yes, and we were hoping you might provide some additional information."

"That was our hope as well."

The walls grew opaque. Jornash stopped at a door and opened it. The trio entered a room of monitors, paper thin and nearly transparent. Various Stuians monitored them, or entered new data via brain wave through an electrode ring sitting on their heads.

Jornash sat before an empty terminal. Windows of code popped up in the air. One window opened with a continual stream of symbols. Jornash pointed at it. "This is the feed for the space station. See this line of data here?" The stream of data froze as if Jornash had taken a picture of it. "What strange code do you see?"

Jeremy scanned the image for a moment before it jumped out at him. "It's all written in a number base code I don't recognize, but the one stream you're pointing to is in binary code."

"Exactly. It isn't ours."

"But how do you know it is from Earth?"

"Allow me to translate into your English." The one binary stream morphed into letters. Most of them appeared to say gibberish, being binary symbols, but one phrase stood out along the lines of nonsense.

Jeremy gasped. "Earth Security Enhancement League."

Jornash turned to face Jeremy. "You know who they are?"

"Not exactly. But I encountered some people in a van who initiated a program called 'subspace.' When we returned to the space station, a new entry on Mickey's superhero list was called 'Captain Subspace.' The patch those men wore had the acronym 'ESEL' on it. But I'd never heard of it before or had a clue what the letters stood for until now."

"Who would you guess they are?"

Jeremy sat in a seat next to Jornash. "I'm getting an idea what they are about, based in part on what happened to us last year and the name."

Jornash's brow wrinkled. "Something happened last year of note?"

"Yes. Long story, but the short version is what we thought was a rogue group in our country's military captured our bodies while we were virtual. They were working on figuring out the virtual connection to the masks and threatened to kill us if I didn't cooperate. I did for a moment, but took the first opportunity to break out. We escaped with our bodies. I then sent messages to our country's leaders and others so they were aware of it and could shut it down. I thought they were done.

"But if their name is any indication, they were the beginning of a planet-wide operation to gain access to the virtual world. I could only guess the goal is to gain this power so they can protect Earth from any alien invasion. I think Lorian's attack must have motivated them to be prepared for future conflicts."

Jornash nodded. "Makes some sense. I think we've underestimated your people's ingenuity. We didn't think they would be able to figure out such advanced technology so quickly. If they gained enough information to develop the ability to tap into the virtual feed and insert programs, it won't be too much longer before they'll start inserting spies and other people."

Jeremy pointed a finger in the air. "But, it would take a good bit of advancing for them to write up a program that would make a human look like a Zorian, and insert them. This Captain Subspace program is their most advanced. But we didn't try it out to discover how advanced."

"Good thing too. Based on this code, had you, it would have fed a lot of data they need back to them to create their own virtual links for themselves. But the next time the new program may not be so obvious."

Bridget, who had been watching the code streams flying by, broke her silence. "Tell him about the phase thingy."

Jornash glanced at Bridget before turning his gaze back to Jeremy, awaiting the explanation.

"When ESEL initiated the subspace program, we experienced a phasing in and out for a couple seconds or so. But nothing happened to us."

Jornash returned to the screen. One window opened with a new code stream. Jornash examined it for a moment. Then he opened another window and checked it out as well. Then two more times the same thing. "Very interesting."

"What?"

"You, Bridget, and Mickey all have the same ESEL stream attached to your feed. But Natalie does not."

Jeremy raised his right eyebrow. "You mean, Natalie's feed is active?"

Jornash nodded.

Bridget giggled. "You can't keep us girls down."

Jeremy shook his head. "I though she was mad enough at me she'd never put that mask back on. Mickey must have calmed her down. Maybe she'll forgive me when we get back."

Jornash said, "Whatever the case, hers is the only feed not contaminated by this code. What is it that is different from her and you three?"

Bridget's hand shot up. "I know, I know!"

"Spit it out, Sis."

"Natalie wasn't with us at the van. Maybe the feed started then? Maybe subspace was more than the new superhero for Mickey."

Jornash shook his head. "Can't be. Some of the changes on Zori happened before the van incident. The feed needed to be in place before that. And you are nowhere near a van right now, yet the feed is connected. There has to be a physical connection, like the helmets and your masks."

Jeremy rubbed his chin. "The only real difference is Natalie just started using her virtual body. Prior to the van incident, she hadn't ever entered the virtual world since the Mind Game ended."

Bridget grunted. "It doesn't make sense. Our bodies are on the space station. How could they have a physical connection with us to keep the feeds going? Did they insert some type of virtual connection into the space station's medical bay? Maybe through the IVs?"

Jeremy thought a second. "You may be onto something, Sis. But not the IVs. Those are real for our real bodies. But something in the bay may be making the connection." He met Jornash's eyes. "How can we tell?"

He turned back to his screen. A window popped open and code poured into it. "The easiest way is to take your bodies back to Earth, and scan for the feed. If the feed goes away, then it is something in the medical bay.

I'm adjusting the programming on Astro Man's gun to scan for this code stream. Just point it at the virtual object and shoot. A reading will appear on the screen. Yes if it is present, no if not."

"That should work." Jeremy paused. "But we can't keep our bodies on Earth. As a matter of fact, for Natalie's safety, we should bring her body to the station too. But not if she will get infected by this feed as well."

Jornash closed the window and turned to Jeremy. "Why can't you keep them on Earth?"

"Too big a risk ESEL will find our bodies and capture them again. We know they can't get to them on Titan."

Bridget brushed her hair back. "Or at least, we thought they couldn't. Until now."

Jeremy sighed. "It might be better to hide her somewhere else. They know too much about Uncle George's place. Once they learn Natalie is going virtual too, they'll capture her."

Jornash shifted uncomfortably in his seat. "Now for the hard news."

Jeremy and Bridget's eyes met. This didn't sound good.

"You recall last time when I said shutting down the virtual machine would be a last resort?"

They both nodded.

"For me, that last resort would be someone taking over the virtual world programming again like Rillian did. We didn't see it coming until it was too late. All we could do is block him from gaining access to our world here. But even though it would mean a loss of the whole Zorian world, I don't want to put them through that again."

Jeremy held out his hand. "But, don't you have the Virtual world stored in computer memories? Can't you just do a reboot if need be?"

Jornash shook his head. "The code is all in computer memory. Unfortunately, the bulk of it is on virtual computers. We didn't have enough room here for the world, just the basic framework. If we shut down the machine, all that code goes bye bye. The Zorians start from scratch on a reboot."

Bridget gasped. "That would be horrible!"

Jornash patted her on the back. "Yes it would. Which is why it is a last resort. However, if your real bodies are on the Titan space station, that means you die if we shut down the machine. We would probably not be able to send you warning in time to get your bodies to Earth."

Jeremy ran his fingers through his hair. "That leaves us with two options. Take our bodies back to Earth and hide them, or—"

"Wouldn't our feeds enable them to locate us?" Bridget interjected.

Jeremy pointed at her. "Good point, Sis, if the feed isn't because our bodies are at the space station. Or, we bring our bodies here. With the masks here, it would be certain they couldn't connect to them being this is all real."

Jornash nodded. "That is why I said we could arrange for you to live here. This would be the safest place for you. If we had to shut down the machine, at least you'd be safe and cared for until we could arrange to get you back."

Jeremy rubbed his chin as he thought. "Appears our plan should be to find out if the foreign code is coming through something inserted into the space station or not. If it is, then we should hide our bodies on Earth somewhere safe and hope they can't find us. If not, and the feed stays connected, then we'll have to come to Zori because they'd be able to locate us no matter where we hid. Once we've done that, we use our superheroes to investigate ESEL, find out how much they know, and figure out how to stop them."

Bridget tossed her hair back. "I say we find out where they're at and go in with guns blazing."

Jornash nodded. "It seems to work for many on your planet."

Jeremy stared at Jornash. "Huh?"

"You know, that Arnold guy." Jeremy continued staring at him as if waiting for more. "The 'I'll be back' guy?"

Jeremy laughed. "Oh, him. Jornash, those are just movies. Not real. In real life, he'd be shot up as soon as he busted the door down. Do you really think all those people shooting at him would miss all the time?"

He flapped one of his flipper-feet. "I assumed only very few people on your planet could use those weapons right. Or maybe most of the people can't see very well. Or—"

"I get the idea." Jeremy sat back in his seat.

"So you're saying it wasn't real?"

"Not even as real as your virtual reality."

"Hum." He smiled. "It was fun to watch, though."

Bridget giggled. "That's the point of movies, silly."

Jeremy stood. "We'd better get back, then. We need to stop Mickey and Natalie from using their superheroes for now, until we figure this out. Ready, Sis?"

She hopped off the chair. "Yep."

"Exit suit," Jeremy said. Blackness over took him.

Chapter 5

Mickey glanced to his right. Natalie had returned to the Black Hole superhero. She studied the details of her new abilities. He found it hard not to stare at her. Not only because she was hot, but because his perception of her had totally changed. He'd pretty much ignored girls up to this point as being not much more than competitors and distractions. Now he couldn't keep his mind off of her.

He forced himself to focus on the monitors. He was supposed to be looking for crime, to right the wrongs of Earth. Now his only concern seemed to be thinking about Natalie. What was wrong with him? Wasn't it only a few months ago he'd shot her for fear that she'd abducted Jeremy? Well, stunned her would be more accurate.

The memory reminded him of Jeremy. He still faced Jeremy finding out about him and Natalie. "Nat, you're going to tell Jeremy as soon as he gets back. Right?" He groaned inside. It was worse than he thought. He'd already given her a nickname.

She turned her head to face him. "Uh? What did you say?"

"Jeremy. You're going to tell Jeremy as soon as he's back. Yes?"

"Oh, yeah. Right. Of course."

"After he tell us what he's learned. He may be too upset to discuss it after you spill the beans."

She smiled. "Sure." Her eyes blinked behind the mask. "Don't worry about it. I'll let him down easy."

Mickey breathed deeply. Why didn't that make him feel better? He focused on the screens, but his mind didn't follow. He stole another view of Natalie. The corner of her mouth lifted. Mickey jerked his head back to the monitors. She had noticed him watching. A scene on one of the monitors caught his eye, and it pulled him back to reality.

He pointed at the monitor. "Look! It is a helicopter out of control. We have to act fast." Mickey fed the coordinates to the suit. "Suit, appear at coordinates as Blue Nova." Darkness swept over him, to be replaced by the skyline of New York City. He stood atop one of the downtown skyscrapers a few blocks from the Empire State Building. Natalie appeared beside him still suited up as Black Hole.

Mickey knocked himself in the head. "You're right. I should have come as G Man. Gravity is more of a factor with this than running fast. You take it."

She nodded and ran to the edge of the roof, but then skidded to a halt. She teetered on the edge before falling off.

"Use your gravity powers to fly."

She shot back into the sky. "Sorry. I froze when I saw how far down it was."

The helicopter spun in circles as it careened toward a skyscraper. Natalie blasted her gravity ray at the falling chopper. It quickly slowed to a halt, hovered for a split second, then shot into the sky like a rocket.

Oh no! She's shot them into space! Mickey flashed forward. The air formed into a solid path under his feet; he ran into the sky. But he could only go so high before the air grew too thin to support him. He gained on the helicopter, but would it be too late? He could feel the air-road growing mushier and mushier.

The chopper approached, but the air-road gave way. Mickey's lift slowed, but not before he caught the bottom rail. He pulled himself up and into the helicopter. The pilot and a camera man from a news crew sat in the seats, eyes wide and cheeks pulled down from the acceleration. Mickey grabbed them under their arms before they knew he was there, zipped out the door, and pushed down from the chopper, which continued to accelerate into the stratosphere. Gravity regained its grip on the trio and pulled them downward.

One of the men had frozen with fear, the other struggled to break free from Blue Nova's grip. Mickey held on tight. The man had to stay with him if he wanted to survive. They plunged into the cumulus cloud peaks and fell through solid white. The man struggled harder, probably thinking the ground was just five seconds away. Mickey could feel him working his way out of his arm. "Stay with me if you want to survive."

Blue Nova churned his feet into a blur; the air-road formed beneath him. He regained traction and zipped toward the ground of New York City. Within seconds, he pulled to a stop on the street beneath where they had first appeared. A watching crowd applauded as Blue Nova laid the two men on the pavement. Medics raced to help them.

"Blue Nova! Where are you?" Natalie's voice echoed over the com.

"Look below you." She turned her head downward; he waved.

"How did you get down there? I feel horrible. I just shot the people in that helicopter into space!"

"I know. I saved them."

"You did not."

"Yes I did."

"How? I didn't see anything."

"Hey, I'm Blue Nova. Need I say more?"

She hit her right palm on the side of her head. "I feel so stupid. I could have killed those people."

"I backed you up, though. Don't feel—" The skyscrapers wavered like they were a reflection in the water and someone had just thrown a stone into it. In three seconds, the feeling passed. Mickey shook his head. "Not again." He scanned the area and located a van parked along the crowded road. The same van as the other night.

"Not again, what?"

"Hold that thought." Should he go after them? Natalie obviously needed more time with her powers before she would be reliable. He'd be going in alone. Exactly what he told Jeremy not to do. Yet, this might be their only chance to find out more about them. If only he could become invisible. A thought came to him. "Suit, appear here as Vulture."

Micky rose into the sky, and once over the van, rained down five homing beacons onto its roof. The van took off and headed down the street. Vulture shot one more homing beacon onto the back bumper for extra measure.

He headed for the top of a skyscraper. "Okay, Black Hole. Time to return to base. Suit, appear as Vulture." The buildings around him vanished to be replaced by the control room. He retracted his wings and landed on the floor. Black Hole appeared beside him.

Mickey ran to a monitor, opened a window, and entered the frequency of his virtual homing signals. A map of New York City appeared upon the screen, with one red, blinking dot moving along a street.

"Who is that?" Natalie leaned over Mickey's shoulder, her chin resting on it.

"That's what I hope to find out. If I'm lucky, Jeremy will return in time so we can both go after them before they discover the homing beacons I put on their van. They're the ones who inserted that rogue program into my list of superheroes. ESEL. Did you feel that phasing in and out when I was standing on the street below you? Like everything wavered as if underwater?"

She shrugged. "No."

Mickey raised an eyebrow. "Really? It was quite pronounced."

"Didn't feel anything of the sort."

"That's odd."

She kissed his neck.

Mickey jerked back. "Natalie!"

"What? Don't you like me anymore?"

Mickey spun around in his seat. "Of course I do. Don't be silly. But don't you see? I almost missed that chopper falling from the sky because I was so . . . ." He paused. "Distracted. I can't get you out of my mind."

She smiled and rubbed his shoulders. "I like that."

"I do too, but we have a responsibility. People almost died because we were distracted."

She sat in the chair next to him. "What am I supposed to do, then? Ignore my feelings?"

Mickey sighed. "I know. I know. I feel the same thing. But we have to separate work from play. Somehow we have to refrain. Besides, Jeremy and Bridget should return sometime today. It's been four days already, which meant they spent at least a full day on Zori. We don't want Jeremy freaking out before you can break it to him all gentle-like and all. So we really need to cool it for now. Avoid touching and acting all in love. Act like nothing has happened."

She cocked her head to the side and frowned. "Really? You think we can pull that off?"

"Just long enough until you can tell Jeremy."

Mickey thought a second. "On the other hand, you're right. I think it is best if you return to your body on Earth. When Jeremy comes back and spills the beans on what he knows, I'll send him down for you to talk to."

She stared at the floor. "You're probably right. Okay." She stood up. "One last kiss?"

Mickey smiled. "Sure." He rose and wrapped her in his arms, and squeezed tightly. He brushed his lips across hers before sinking into a well of fresh excitement. The skin of her bare back rubbed against his hands like fine silk. "Until we meet again." He released her.

She waved, then said, "Exit, suit." She vanished.

Mickey collapsed into the chair. What a mess. He returned his attention to the beacon. The van had stopped. Mickey saved a capture of the screen for the coordinates. He sat back in his chair. He wanted Jeremy to come, but dreaded it all the same. Why did he feel so guilty if it was right? And why did it also feel so right too?

Mickey shook his head. "Women."

Jeremy opened his eyes to the ceiling of the medical bay. He reached over and disconnected his IV. He stretched and pushed himself upright. Bridget already stirred on her bed. Jeremy slid off his perch and stretched his legs. "Welcome back to reality, Sis." He scanned the area for anything that appeared out of place, though he had no idea what he was hoping to find.

She landed on the floor. "Reality, such as it is. I'm going to get some food."

Jeremy called after her. "Grab me something too. Anything, doesn't matter, and meet me in the control room."

"Okay." She exited the room. The doors slid closed behind her.

Jeremy worked his way out of the medical bay, down the hall, and into the control room. Mickey sat at a chair all alone, watching the monitors. Jeremy scanned the room. "Hi Mick."

Mickey spun around. His mouth feigned a smile, but his face had lost all color. "Hi, Bucko. Glad to have you back."

Jeremy stopped before him. "Mick, you look like you've seen a ghost. Are you alright?"

"I . . . well . . ." He glanced at a monitor showing a map of a city. "I guess I sort of did. I ran into ESEL again. Had the phase thing zap me."

Jeremy sat in the chair next to him. "Did you get any new superheroes?"

"None that I've found. Who knows what they did this time. But the odd thing is Natalie didn't experience the phase shift."

Jeremy raised an eyebrow. "Natalie went on a mission?"

Mickey nodded.

"With you?"

Mickey frowned. "What's so hard to believe about that? It was quite normal, I assure you."

Jeremy slapped Mickey on the arm. "Lighten up, bud. It's just you two have had such an antagonistic relationship. I was surprised to see her feed running in the virtual world stream."

Mickey's jaw dropped. "You saw her feed? I mean, like, how much of it did you see? What could you do? Look through her eyes or something?"

Jeremy stared at Mickey a moment before answering. He'd rarely seen happy, go lucky Mickey act like he was about to be convicted before a judge. "What might I have seen if I could have?"

Mickey stared at the monitor. "Nothing but some friendly banter. Not that we talked all that much. I mean, she kept me company. But just general chit chat. I helped her explore a couple of her superheroes, stuff like that."

"Where is Natalie?"

"She exited the virtual world. Once you catch me up on stuff, you should go see her."

Jeremy leaned forward. "So, she's okay? Everything is back to normal?"

Mickey sucked in a breath. "I wouldn't classify it as normal. You'll just need to talk to her."

"Okay, but first we need to run a quick test."

Mickey's color returned to his face as he pointed at a red blinking dot on the map. "I think first we need to check this out before we lose them, if we already haven't. As Vulture, I put some homing beacons on the ESEL van before it drove away."

"Cool. We can kill two birds with one stone. We need to go to Earth to perform the test. But we need to do it in your real body. We need to take it to Earth."

"Won't that be risky?"

Jeremy nodded. "Yes. But it is the only way to find out whether we can hide on Earth or not. We can't keep our bodies at the space station any longer."

Mickey wrinkled his brow. "We can't? Why not?"

"I'll explain later. Right now, I'll become Astro Man, we'll take his ship carrying your body to Earth. Once there, you'll stay inside the ship and become whatever. Only, stick with superheroes you've used. No new ones."

Mickey nodded. "Sir, yes, sir!" He stood up. "Exit, suit." Mickey vanished.

Jeremy ran his fingers through his hair.

Bridget entered the control room, staring

back over her shoulders. "What's with Mickey. He's acting weird."

"No, that's the problem. He's not acting weird like Mick." His gut said something was wrong. Mickey wasn't telling him the whole truth. He'd never sensed deception from Mickey before.

Chapter 6

The cloaked Astro Jet entered Earth's atmosphere. Mickey sat in the back seat, saying little over the one hour and fifteen minute trip from Titan to Earth. That fact caused Jeremy even more concern. Mickey was not acting like himself.

Jeremy glanced at the beacon signal as the reentry flames rushed over the ship's shielding. Jeremy readjusted course to intersect with the beacons. They sank through the clouds until the white gave way to a blue ocean, and in the distance loomed New York City. Jeremy could make out the small island where the Statue of Liberty stood.

"Hey, Mick. You awake?"

"Huh?" Mickey shuffled behind him. "Yeah. I'm awake."

"We're almost there." Within seconds, they flew over the tops of skyscrapers. They followed the signals into the outer areas of the city. Jeremy pointed down to the ground. "Over there. The signal says the beacons are there."

Mickey leaned forward to the window. "An empty field?"

"It appears so."

Jeremy flew over the field to be sure. No van, but the signals did come from there. He sat the ship down in the field and popped the hatch. "Use your mask to appear here."

Mickey pulled his mask out and slid it on. "Appear here as Vulture." Mickey dropped off unconscious, and Vulture materialized beside the ship.

Astro Man pulled out his gun, changed to the new settings, and raised the gun.

Mickey flinched. "Why are you pointing that at me?"

Jeremy eyed his sights at Mickey. "I'll tell you in a moment. I need to find out something."

Mickey's jaw dropped open and he jerked from side to side. "No, really, it wasn't my fault! I didn't intend for anything to happen. I —"

"Calm down and hold still. This won't hurt a bit."

Mickey dropped to his knees and raised his hands is if prayer to Jeremy. "I'm so sorry. Really I am. But surely it's not worth this! Don't kill me for my sins!"

Jeremy squeezed the trigger. A click from the gun caused Mickey to fall the ground, his hand over his heart. At least Mickey was acting a bit more normal now. He checked the screen. It read "Yes." Jeremy stomped on the ground. "Blasted ESEL! Their feed link is still there."

Mickey split his fingers apart and stared at Jeremy through them. "You're not going to kill me?"

Jeremy bopped Mickey on the head. "Quit playing around. We've some serious decisions to make about where to keep our bodies. There might be only one option left."

Mickey wrapped his arms around Jeremy's legs. "Oh, thank you so much. You're the best friend I could ever have. Slow to anger and merciful to the sinner!"

Jeremy yanked Mickey up by the arm. "Mick, seriously. Focus on the task at hand. Collect the beacons. Make sure you have them all, and if not, see if you can find the missing one's signal." Jeremy released Mickey."

Mickey dusted himself off. "So you forgive me?" He started going through the grass, picking up beacons.

"Forgive you for what?"

"Uh . . . well, for leading you on this goose chase."

"Don't be silly. It's not like you did anything wrong trying to track them."

"Yeah. Nothing wrong. Nothing at all." He picked up another. "That's all of them. Six in all."

Jeremy nodded. "Well then, let's get back to the base, and we'll meet with everyone so I only have to explain this once. But until further notice, no more missions."

"But people will die."

"I know, but it can't be helped. Until we can sort this out, the world will be like it was two years ago, with no superheroes to save them, other than the ones on comic book pages saving people from boredom."

Mickey breathed deep and nodded. "Exit suit." Vulture vanished. Inside the ship, Mickey pulled his mask off.

Jeremy hopped into Astro Man's ship, closed the hatch, and blasted off. He shook his head as they flew into space. Could life get any more complicated? He didn't see how.

———

Mickey leaned back in Uncle George's couch. "So, you're saying we need to take our real bodies to Zori?"

Jeremy rubbed his chin. "For you, me, and Bridget, it is the only place we're safe from ESEL. They can't get to us in the Stuian's underwater building, because it's real and protected. It is the only place left from which we can operate virtually without the ESEL code piggybacking onto our feeds."

Jeremy pointed at Natalie. "She, however, doesn't have that code in her feed. We figured because ESEL doesn't know about her yet. She could hide out somewhere on Earth. We'd be eventually located, and our bodies stolen again while we were virtual thanks to the ESEL code. That's why I brought your body to Earth, Mick. So I could see if there was some link to the station or not. Unfortunately, it appears the code feed is not coming from a location on the station."

Mickey threw up his hands. "From where then? There would have to be some connection to our bodies. We'd have to be plugged into it in some way."

Jeremy nodded. "That's what Jornash said. That's why we thought maybe it had something to do with the station since our bodies were there and Natalie's is not."

"But they know about me now." Natalie lifted her head. "They would have seen me in action when we saved the people crashing in the helicopter."

"She's right," Mickey said. "And this would be the first place they look. We've got to get her out of here before they put two and two together."

"And Uncle George too," Bridget added. "Isn't he in danger?"

All eyes turned to Uncle George. He cleared his throat. "No need to worry about me. I've got a cabin in the mountains I can spend a few months in. Remember? I'm used to living alone. This past nearly two years has been an exception."

Bridget smiled. "But an exception you've grown attached to. Yes?"

He laughed. "Most definitely. I would miss

you all. But Natalie could come with me. It would make a good hiding place."

Jeremy turned to Natalie. She stared at the floor. "What do you think, Natalie? Either way might be a risk."

Bridget raised a hand. "But, what if the Sutians shut down the virtual machine? We'd be trapped on Zori. Right?"

Jeremy met her eyes. "That is one of the risks going to Zori, though I don't see we have much choice." He returned to Natalie. "What do you say, Natalie?"

She glanced at Mickey before staring at the floor again. Her hair dangled over her head so Jeremy couldn't see her face. "I'll have to think about it."

"You don't have long to think about it, Nat . . . alie." Mickey swallowed and stared out the window as if afraid of something.

"Mick's right," Jeremy said. "You can't stay here tonight. We need to leave today."

Natalie raised her head and met Jeremy's eyes. Her down-turned lips and drooping eyes told Jeremy something was very wrong.

She said, "Can we talk in private?"

"Sure." He rose from his chair.

Natalie glanced at Mickey, who still stared out the window, then proceeded to follow Jeremy down the hall to his room. They entered and shut the door.

Jeremy sat on the edge of his bed. "Okay, what's wrong?"

Natalie pulled out a chair from the desk and sat. She placed her hands over her face and heaved. Jeremy patiently waited. He wanted to comfort her, but she'd created a purposeful distance by sitting away from him. As if she didn't want him to reach her.

She sucked in a deep breath and held her head up. "I was so angry at you when you left me."

"Mick explained that, though, didn't he?"

She nodded. "Oh yes. He explained it well enough. I still felt angry though. Distant from you. As if you no longer cared. No longer loved me."

"And now?"

She shook for a moment, then leaped from her chair, rushed across the room, and landed on Jeremy. Her arms wrapped around him and pushed him back onto the bed. "I know you love me. And I love you so much. Can you ever forgive me?"

Jeremy rubbed her back. "I don't feel I need to forgive you. You need to forgive me for being so heartless. I could have found a better way of handling that."

She raised her head and drew her lips to his. Her gentle kiss reminded Jeremy of all they'd been through together. First on Zori, then on Similaris. She released his lips but not his heart. Then she gave Jeremy a tight hug before lifting herself into a sitting position on the edge of the bed.

She smiled. "Of course I've forgiven you. But I am confused."

Jeremy sat up. "About what?"

"Going to Zori. On one hand, I want to be with you. It would make sense for us to stick together. Uncle George would be better off not having me around to attract more trouble for him. And if you were stranded on Zori, I'd rather be there with you than separated forever on Earth."

Jeremy smiled and kissed her. "That's so sweet of you to say."

"On the other hand, I suck at this superhero business. I almost shot two men into space. If it hadn't been for Mickey saving them, they'd probably be orbiting Mars by now."

Jeremy rubbed her back, glad she was feeling closer to him now. "You'll learn. You just have to get used to your powers."

She met his eyes. "I fear I'll be more of a burden and distraction than a help. Everyone will have to be cleaning up after me."

Jeremy shrugged. "I'm used to you being a distraction." He squeezed her in a side hug.

She smiled. "Well, I do have a confession."

Foreboding echoed in Jeremy's thoughts. "I'm listening."

She breathed deep. "Like I said, I was pretty upset with you, and feeling distant from you. Mickey came and told me what had happened, and comforted me."

Jeremy nodded. "I did tell him to do that. And to make sure you knew I loved you."

"He did tell me that. But I couldn't feel it. Actions speak louder than words, and all that. Well, I was thankful for his help. He did help me to get over my anger and agree to go back into the virtual world. So, in the heat of the moment, I did something which seemed not a big deal at the time, but in retrospect wasn't a good idea." She breathed in a couple times and stared at the floor. "I gave him a thankfulness kiss. On the lips." She turned her eyes upon Jeremy.

Jeremy stared into her eyes. Was he losing her? It didn't seem like it. Yet. . . "Is that all you felt? Thankfulness?"

"Like I said, that's all I meant it to be."

"But that's not all it became, I take it. Thank you kisses are on the cheek." Jeremy braced himself.

"I know. I know! Like I said, I was in a bad state, feeling distant from you, and suddenly close to Mickey in the moment. I went too far."

Jeremy's heart pumped hard. Her answer to the next question could be critical. "So, is that where it ended?"

She shook her head. "That's what I hadn't

planned on. I didn't realize how much that simple kiss would affect Mickey. He suddenly became obsessed with me. He kept staring at me. Finding opportunities to touch me. And while I didn't think of him that way, due to the state of my mind, I didn't do much to discourage him. Except when it came down to it, I said this couldn't happen. That I loved you, and a relationship between us would never work. I don't think he's over me yet."

Jeremy let his shoulders slump. "So did anything more happen?"

"He kissed me one other time. I pushed him away. Said I didn't want to destroy our friendship or hurt you."

"I can't believe Mick would do that. After all our years of friendship."

She put her arm around Jeremy's shoulders. "Don't blame him. I should have never kissed him on the lips. It's as if I turned on his hormones and he couldn't help himself."

Jeremy smiled. "I know what that feels like."

"And you know Mickey. He's impulsive."

Jeremy laughed. "Boy do I know! He's the epitome of acting before you think, sometimes."

She reached over and kissed Jeremy. "So don't be hard on him. He values your friendship and is worried how this will effect it. I know he doesn't want to hurt you either. His hormones got away from him is all."

"This does explain his strange behavior when I returned. But don't worry. I'll let him know I forgive him and harbor no bad feelings toward him."

Natalie hugged Jeremy again. Her lips met his, and her love flooded his soul. She sat back. "You're so caring. I knew you'd do the right thing. But now you see my problem. I wouldn't just be a distraction to you, but to him as well. Might be best if I stay with Uncle George, or maybe return to Chicago."

Jeremy stood up. "No, I don't think so. If you are both to remain my friends, you'll have to learn to get along with the distraction. When Mick puts his mind to it, he can work through it. He'll just have to get over it. And he can't do that if you're not there for him to get over."

Jeremy fixed his eyes on her. "He knows it is over, right?"

"Yes and no. I mean, I've made it clear, but he apparently can't shut down so easily. It's like I lit a fire that he's having trouble putting out. But with you back, that should change things."

He didn't like the sound of that. He'd forgive Mickey, but they would have to have a heart-to-heart talk. "So, you're coming to Zori?"

She stood and hugged him. "Your arguments have won me over. I'll come to Zori with you three."

Jeremy grinned. "Good. I'd hate to be there without you." He pushed his lips into hers, thankful the worst had not happened, and she still loved him. He'd think twice about leaving her so dejected again.

The door to the room slammed open. Mickey jumped into the room. "Jeremy! We've got to . . ." His face froze at seeing the two of them locked into a kiss.

Jeremy turned toward him. The shock on Mickey's face appeared to be more than hormones.

Mickey slapped himself. "We have to get Natalie out of here. ESEL is here!"

Chapter 7

"Here? How do you know?" Jeremy's heart pounded.

"Helicopters are landing outside."

Jeremy froze. What could they do?

Mickey said, "Suit, appear here as Blue Nova." His form disappeared and reappeared as Blue Nova. "I can speed her and Uncle George away. You and Bridget exit now."

Jeremy paused. Was it a good idea to leave him alone with Natalie again?

Bridget rushed in behind Mickey. "We've got to go now, BJ."

Jeremy huffed. "Alright. Take them both. Let us know where you're at, and we'll return with a ship to pick her up."

Mickey turned his back toward Natalie. "Hop on piggyback, and hold on." Natalie climbed onto his back. She glanced at Jeremy before Mickey sped off into a blur to get Uncle George and escape.

Jeremy gritted his teeth. "Could things get any worse? I've got to learn to keep my mouth shut."

"BJ! Now!"

He nodded. "Exit suit." He heard her repeat it as he vanished into the void.

————

"Uncle George. What direction is your cabin?" Mickey held the man in his arms. He probably looked ridiculous, a teen boy holding a big man in his arms and a woman clinging to his back. But he'd become accustom to looking ridiculous.

Uncle George pointed. "Cabin's across the valley and on the other mountain."

"You two hang on. Here we go." Mickey shot out the back door, after Uncle George opened it for him. The air-road solidified under Mickey's feet; he zipped into the sky and headed toward the mountain Uncle George had pointed to.

Mickey spun in a circle to check what ESEL was doing. Men exited the helicopters and entered Uncle George's house. Good, they hadn't spotted them leaving. Mickey raced to the mountain and settled upon a ledge. "Which way, Uncle?"

"See that outcropping over there?"

Mickey nodded.

"My cabin is just on the other side of it."

Mickey zipped off the ledge and stood in front of the cabin within a second.

Uncle George slid out of Mickey's hands. "I'll go get the fire started and something cooking." He unlocked the door to the cabin and entered.

Natalie dropped to the ground and put a hand on Mickey's shoulder. "I can explain."

Mickey spun around. "I can't stay here. They'll lock onto my location in a few minutes. But to paraphrase a famous Jedi . . ." He passed his hand, palm down, in front of his chest. "This is not the clean break I was looking for." He opened his mouth to say more.

Natalie placed her hand over his mouth. "There's a reason to my madness. I realized right now, with all that is going on, the last thing Jeremy needs is to deal with this on top of it all. He needs to focus on solving this problem, and saving Zori . . . again. After this is done, then I can tell him the whole truth."

Mickey wrinkled his brow. "Whole truth? What did you tell him?"

She sighed. "He knows I kissed you and that we kissed one other time. I convinced him that I encouraged you, and you weren't at fault. But he doesn't know about the rest of it."

Mickey stomped his foot on the ground. "Fine! Now I've got a big secret to keep from my best friend. Exactly the position I didn't want to be in."

She bowed her head. "I'm sorry."

Mickey waved his head from side to side. "Oh, this is just complicated. But I really do need to get out of here. The longer I wait, the bigger the risk you'll be discovered." He reached over and kissed her.

She enveloped him in her arms and held it for a few seconds before releasing him. "See you in an hour or so. I'm coming to Zori."

He smiled. "Good."

"And don't divulge any info to Jeremy. We have to wait until this is over."

He breathed deep and nodded. "Exit suit."

————

Jeremy stood in the mess hall, packing food. Bridget worked on packing other supplies. Mickey walked into the mess hall. "I'm back. Natalie and Uncle George are safe."

Jeremy continued filling the container with food. "Sis, why don't you go get the IV equipment and put it into the Eagle VI?"

She set the bag of supplies on the counter. "Okay. Can't wait to be on Zori in person again. And to stay with the Overlords . . ." She slapped her hands on each side of her cheeks. "Oh my!" She giggled as she skipped out the door.

Mickey laughed. "Well, she's happy."

Jeremy turned to face Mickey. He gripped

the side of the counter. "Mick, what were you thinking?"

His head dropped. "I know. I wasn't."

"I thought I knew you better than that. To take advantage of a woman when she's vulnerable."

Mickey's head snapped up. "Vulnerable!" He opened his mouth to say more, but he froze.

"Yes. She was angry at me for leaving. I entrusted her to your care. Not to replace me."

"She . . . I mean, I tried . . . well . . ." Mickey stared blankly at Jeremy.

Jeremy raised his palms toward Mickey. "I know. She told me about that kiss of thanking you. Apparently that ended up being more than intended."

Mickey gazed at the floor. "You can say that again."

Jeremy approached him and placed a hand on Mickey's shoulder. "Look, I know how it feels when you get all giddy with excitement over a girl. It can consume you. You know how crazy I've acted over Natalie before."

Mickey raised his head and cracked a smile.

"But you've got to get a hold of yourself. Natalie loves me and I love her. She doesn't need any distractions worrying about what you are going to do."

"Her? Distracted?"

Jeremy held out a hand. "I know, you're distracted as well, dealing with the feelings she stirred up in you. But look, I forgive you. Let's drop this so we can focus on dealing with ESEL. But you'll have to learn how to deal with your passions."

Mickey smiled. "I'm really sorry, Bucko. You're right." He reached out to take Jeremy's hand, but instead pulled him into a hug. "Remember, Bucko, no matter what things look like on the outside, I'm totally behind you. Our friendship comes before any woman."

Jeremy patted Mickey on the back before letting him go. "Deal. Now, let's get this done so we can kick some ESEL butt."

"You've got it." Mickey held up a finger. "I did have a thought on the virtual feed connection."

Jeremy returned to packing. "What's that?"

"Remember last year, when they captured our bodies?"

"How could I forget?"

"What if they implanted something into our bodies, so it isn't obvious?"

Jeremy let the bag of bars in his hand fall on the counter. "That's brilliant, Mick. I should have thought of that."

"But you didn't." Mickey grinned. "The amazing Mick has returned."

"Let's check it out. To the medical bay."

They passed Bridget in the hall carrying several pieces of equipment. "Hey, I could use some help here." They ignored her and entered the medical bay.

Mickey lay down on the bed. "Wouldn't the medical robots have detected anything like that by now?"

"Not likely. They have to be told what to notice. I doubt finding implanted pieces of equipment is on their standard list." Jeremy called out, "Medical robot."

The spherical robot, several arms extending off of it, floated toward Jeremy. "State your request," echoed from it in a tin-like, male voice.

"Scan Mickey's body for any implants or foreign substances."

It hovered over Mickey's body. "Activating scan." A light flashed across Mickey's body several times before the robot responded. "Scans detect no implants or foreign substances in the subject's body."

Mickey banged his hand on the side of the bed. "Blast it all. I was sure that would be it."

"Me too. I can't think of anything else that makes sense."

Bridget entered the room.

Mickey dropped his feet onto the floor. "Time to get moving to Zori."

Bridget planted her hands on her hips. "Yeah, and some help you've been."

Jeremy grabbed his new watch sitting on a shelf and put it on.

"I was wondering when you might use that. I thought maybe you'd forgotten about it."

Jeremy feigned surprise. "Why Sis, when would I ever do that?"

She grabbed a bag. "Just get that equipment beside you and follow me, soldier."

Jeremy and Mickey saluted. "Sir, yes sir."

"Puleze!" She walked out the door.

Jeremy grabbed the IV equipment.

"I had another thought, Bucko," Mickey said.

"Yes?"

He frowned. "This is just a thought. I'm not saying it is true. But when you said Natalie's virtual feed didn't have the ESEL code piggy-backed on it, it made me think of when she was in the Mind Game. Remember, I suspected something to begin with. What if she isn't who she appears to be?"

"But you verified she was real, that her mask was off. She didn't say she was taken over. Right?"

Mickey stared at the ceiling. "I don't know. Like I said, it may be totally off. Just, she's not acting like herself."

"Did you notice some odd behavior while I was gone?"

"Yes, you could say that."

"Like what?"

"Well . . ." Mickey stared at a bed as if he

was thinking about lying down. "You sort of had to be there to get it. It's just, her attitude toward me, toward us, isn't the same since she put on that mask."

Jeremy ran his fingers through his hair. "Are you suggesting the mask actually changed something in her brain?"

"It's just a theory. But yes. You said Holbreth gave you that mask? Did he say who he received it from?"

"No. I assumed the Stuians created it like they did ours." Jeremy widened his eyes. "If ESEL somehow created that mask and had it get to Holbreth, her mask wouldn't need a piggybacked code."

Mickey threw up his hand. "But if they are just now figuring out how to insert simpler program codes into the virtual world, could we expect them to build the equivalent of virtual helmets? If they could do that, they'd have a virtual army on Zori already."

A quiver ran up Jeremy's spine. "Let's pray that isn't true. But I think one of the first things we need to do once on Zori is to have Jornash check her mask. Make sure it is one of theirs, and not ESEL's."

Bridget popped her head in the door. "I thought you guys were in a hurry? Are we going or not?"

Jeremy headed toward the door with Mickey in tow. "Let's get underway before we're flogged or something."

———

Jeremy watched as Earth grew smaller against the star-studded blackness of space. For all he knew, this could be the last time he'd ever see it, much less set foot on it again. He pulled his eyes off the rear monitor and focused on the vastness of space ahead as the moon zipped by.

Jeremy laughed. "Mick, do you know how long it took the first astronauts to travel from Earth to the Moon?"

"Yeah. Three days."

"And here we are, traveling to another galaxy in our universe in a little over one day."

Mickey grinned. "The wonders of virtual space ships."

"And a well placed worm hole."

The cabin door slid open. Jeremy and Mickey turned to see who had entered. Natalie stood in the doorway.

She gazed at the controls and out the view port. "This does bring back memories. Not good ones either. It's like remembering a dream you had once." She caressed a wall. "No, more like a nightmare."

She stepped up behind Jeremy and placed her hand on his shoulder.

Jeremy patted her hand. "Are you going to be alright?"

She squeezed his shoulder. "Yes. I think so. It's just, a very odd feeling. Especially knowing I'm here in the flesh, not a virtual body." She reached down and gave Jeremy a quick kiss.

Jeremy glanced at Mickey. He studied something on the control panel, pretending not to notice. Then Jeremy realized something. Something important. "Why didn't I think about that?"

"About what?" Natalie asked.

"Mick. Take a good look at Natalie."

Mickey continued focusing on the controls. "I know what she looks like."

"No, look at her, but look at her as a Zorian would. What do you see?"

Mickey huffed, but then turned to stare at Natalie. His chin quivered a moment, but then his eyes grew wide. "The dead woman who deceived them!"

"Right. Holbreth knows the truth, but most

Zorians don't. She was on the station for a little while when we returned from Similaris, but most Zorians don't have a clue that Natalie isn't, well, the Natalie they knew. They'll think she has returned from the dead to haunt them or something."

"Well, I can't stay locked up in this ship forever."

"Bucko." Mickey waved a hand in front of Jeremy's face. "That could be a problem if we go prancing around Zori, but we aren't. We're staying with the Stuians."

"Ah, yeah. You're right. Psych!"

Natalie swatted Jeremy on the back of the head. "You guys. I'm going to keep Bridget company, but let me know when we're getting close to the worm hole. Those are cool to watch." She exited the room.

The beeps of the ship's systems and the hum of its engines echoed in the background.

"Bucko?"

"Yes, Mick."

"We never did figure out what that last phase shift I experienced did to the virtual world. It must have been something big."

Jeremy rocked his chair back. "Like I said. They aren't likely to make it obvious. And we weren't there to hear what they called the program they inserted. We'll just have to watch out for anything out of the ordinary."

Mickey rubbed his face with his palms. "Like anything has been ordinary lately."

Jeremy didn't say anything. But the last two years hadn't been ordinary. Being superheroes had its cool factor, but this continual dealing with reality as not real had grown tiresome. He was ready to hang up his mask. The best way to stop ESEL was to give the mask back to the Stuians, and have them ship the four of them back to Earth, and pray ESEL hadn't already developed their own virtual helmet or mask.

"Mick, are we on auto pilot?"

"Course laid in for the worm hole and Zori. Not much input from us needed. Sensors will let us know if any objects come within range of hitting us."

Jeremy rose from the chair. "Then I want to call a meeting to order. I have a proposition to make." And he hoped they would agree to it, though he didn't feel he could force them too. But he also had another reason to suggest this option. If Natalie was someone other than Natalie, it might flush that fact into the open.

"What's the meeting about, Bucko?"

"A solution to stop ESEL dead in their tracks. But it will take all of us cooperating to do it." Jeremy smiled. He was so ready to get his normal life back. Even if it meant an hour's drive down Uncle George's mountain to go to school every day.

Chapter 8

Natalie settled into a chair around the conference table in the mess hall. "Okay, what's up?"

Jeremy checked everyone's eyes around the table before proceeding. "I have a proposition for you. We all need to agree to do this if we do it. One person says no, and it won't work. But I have a way to shut down ESEL and the threat to Zori."

Bridget's eyes lit up. "That would be a good thing."

"It will mean some sacrifice on our part, however. We know that ESEL is using our masks to gain access to the virtual world, and have already done some minor test runs. But so far, there's no evidence they also have developed masks to enter the virtual world, since they are piggybacking on our feeds.

"We are currently in route to Zori in our real bodies, carrying our masks. I'm proposing that we give the masks back to the Stuians and ask them to destroy them. Then send us back to Earth. Without our masks, we are not worth the time of day to ESEL, Zori will be safe from them, and we can go back to living our normal lives." Jeremy smiled at Natalie.

Mickey raised his hand. "Good idea, but there is one big negative. What about all the people's lives we could help if we stay superheroes?

Jeremy knew Mickey had a big heart, and from time to time he showed it. "That will be unfortunate. But look at it this way, Mick. Our becoming superheroes was a fluke. Something none of us could have ever predicted. By all rights, the numerous people whose lives we have saved and affected should be dead and damaged by now. But they aren't because we've been playing superhero for the past year and a half. Can we really ask the Zorians to sacrifice their whole culture to save some people on Earth from events that would have happened anyway?"

Mickey shook his head. "Fluke or no fluke, it did happen. We have this power." He paused and bowed his head. "But you're right. I can't ask the Zorians to do that." He breathed in. "I'll do it."

Jeremy turned to Bridget.

Bridget blinked her eyes. "No more Comet Girl and Rainbow Girl?"

"That's what it would mean. You'd be Bridget and only Bridget."

She smiled. "No, I would be the sister of the most compassionate and loving brother ever! Of course I'd do it if it helps the Zorians."

Jeremy met Natalie's eyes.

She cleared her throat. "Can't say I've become attached to my hero personas just yet. Not had as much time as you have. And I've wondered if I'm really cut out for this superhero stuff. I mean, you have the power to do good, yes. But there is also the power to mess up, to kill people, even accidentally. I'm not sure I can live with that."

Natalie placed her right palm down in the center of the table. "I'm in."

Mickey and Bridget placed their palms over Natalie's. Jeremy grinned and placed his hand over them. "Let it be done, then. I'll talk to Jornash about it when we arrive on Zori."

Bridget sat up straight. "Good. Now, can we eat? I'm starving."

Jeremy yawned as his body began to wake up. He focused on the ceiling, and recalled he lay in the Eagle VI, flying to Zori. It was one thing to be in this ship knowing you were virtual, but to think that his body was in a galaxy millions of light years from Earth was hard to accept. Flying there in a virtual ship, no less. Though he frequently forgot it was virtual, it seemed so real.

Jeremy sat up and yawned again, stretching his arms and legs as he did. Then exited his cabin. The short hallway leading to the sleeping quarters was empty. He made his way to the control room. The doors slid open. Natalie stood behind Mickey's chair as he sat in it.

Natalie jerked back and spun around. "Oh, good morning sleepy head."

Mickey glanced over his shoulders. "Just showing her the controls. In case she needs to fly this thing at some point. You never know."

Jeremy yawned again and said through it, "Not a bad idea. Glad you're staying on top of things. Anyone brewed some coffee?"

Natalie laughed. "How quickly you forget? Packets are in the mess hall."

Mickey said, "You may want to wait on that. We'll be landing in a few minutes."

Jeremy squinted out the view port. An orange ball, about the size of a dime, slowly grew among the stars. "Cool. I think I'll change clothes and get some coffee anyway. Natalie, coming with me?"

She glanced at Mickey and smiled at Jeremy. "Sure."

They left the control room and then entered the mess hall. Jeremy pulled out a coffee packet, broke the seal, and extended the straw. He could feel it heating up in his hand.

Jeremy sipped as Natalie seated herself.

"Do you think it's a good idea to encourage him like that?"

She shrugged. "I woke and went to the bathroom. I heard him talking to himself. Figured he could use the company."

"But you know how much you've affected him. You don't want to make this any harder for him than it already is."

She stared at the table top. "We have an understanding. He didn't try anything. He knows better."

"All the same, you're torturing him doing that. It's like dangling candy in front of a kid and then pulling it away at the last moment. That's just mean. I would prefer you limit any alone time with him to whatever is absolutely necessary and no more. For his sake."

She nodded. "I guess you're right. Not being a man, I forget about those kinds of things."

Jeremy slurped up the last of the coffee. "And being a woman, you'd best get dressed yourself. Unless you expect to meet the Stuians in your night gown."

She laughed. "Yes, I guess I'd better." She rose from her chair and pulled him to her in a hug. Then planted a long kiss on his lips. "See you in a bit."

Jeremy nodded and watched her float out of the mess hall. Her loving kiss echoed through his body. But somewhere, deep down, something felt wrong. At least she seemed willing enough to give up the virtual life in the meeting, so he didn't expect she was being used by ESEL. Still, something was out of whack. If only he could place his finger on it. He stuffed the empty bag into a trash bin and shot his way out the door.

After cleaning up and putting on fresh clothes, Jeremy returned to the control room. Mickey guided the ship through the clouds of

Zori. The barren landscape below held small bodies of water here and there, and virtual cities dotted the countryside, some quite big. If the Stuians turned off the virtual machine, all those cities and Zorians would disappear. The Zorians would return to their blobs of goo sitting around the landscape. To imagine Holbreth being one of them seemed silly. But that was a real possibility. A fear he would never have to face, that each Zorian did.

Natalie and Bridget entered the room. Bridget clapped her hands. "We're almost there." She hit a button on the wall and a seat folded down. She hopped in and snapped the belt into place.

Natalie followed Bridget's example. "I guess since Mickey's driving, belting in is a good idea."

Mickey huffed. "You'll not be able to tell when we're down, I promise."

Natalie chuckled. "I recall a certain pilot getting sick while I drove you through the canyon leading to this lake."

"That wasn't sickness." Mickey mumbled something. "I was merely experiencing turbulence after-effects."

Jeremy put a hand on Mickey's shoulder. "How about focusing on driving and make sure we don't need these belts?"

Mickey stared straight ahead and raised his shoulders. "Focusing."

Rocky mountains flew under the ship until a canyon emerged from the mass of peaks and valleys. Mickey adjusted course to follow it. Within two minutes, a lake appeared nestled between the mountains. Mickey slowed the Eagle down and guided it to the shore of the lake.

The four exited the space ship and stood by the water, waves gently lapping against the rocks. Natalie held Jeremy's hand. "Are you sure this is safe?"

"Oh yes. We've done this many times."

Bridget laughed. "It's fun. Don't you remember?"

Natalie stared at the water. "I never did go to see the Stuians. Don't you remember?"

"Yeah, I remember now. You knew you'd be found out if you went in there, so you avoided going in with us."

"The Zorian that took over my virtual body knew that. I didn't know anything at the time. Just watched like a spectator."

Jeremy stepped into the water and pulled Natalie behind him. "Come on. The tubes are activated by you being in the water a little ways."

Bridget ran out into the water. Mickey followed them. When the water reached Bridget's waist, a bubbling erupted on the surface ten feet in front of her. A big tube broke the surface of the water, rose into the air, arced back down, and fell upon Bridget who reached for it. The tube pulled back into the air and sank under the waves.

Natalie pulled back on Jeremy's hand. "I'm not so sure about that."

"Believe me, you'll enjoy it."

"But, it looked like it swallowed her whole."

Jeremy held both hands. "Have I ever steered you wrong?"

Another tube shot into the air and came down to suck Mickey into its jaws. Natalie swallowed. "Well . . ." She smiled. "Not really."

"Let's do this together. I'll stand over there, and you go a little beside me."

She nodded, but kept her lips tightly together.

Jeremy almost laughed at the difference. The last time they were here, Natalie was a confident, fear nothing, hard-nosed ball of fire, ready to take on anything. Now, she appeared scared of everything. The difference a Zorian body-snatcher can make.

She stepped a few paces to the side and they both walked out together. In a few seconds, two tubes flew into the air and came down upon them. Jeremy heard Natalie scream until the tube covered her, and Jeremy disappeared into his own tube.

After flowing through the turns and twist of the tube, Jeremy splashed into a pool of water. As he pulled himself out, Natalie stood up in her pool, frowning.

Natalie sloshed onto the floor. "Fun? Really?" She pointed at her hair dripping with water. "Do you know how long I spent fixing up my hair?"

Bridget shook her head. "It dries."

Jornash stood by the door. "Glad you all could make it. Follow me."

Natalie walked beside Jeremy as they watched fish swimming around the building. "This place is pretty amazing. Staying here wouldn't be the worst thing to happen to us."

Jeremy squeezed her hand, but didn't say anything. They entered the code room where rows of computers and screens lined the area. Jornash stopped at an open terminal and began entering commands through the ring on his head.

Jeremy figured this would be as good time as any. "Jornash, we're prepared to make a proposition I think will fix all this. We are going to turn our masks into you and you can take us back to Earth. No more superheroes. You can shut down the Titan space station reality. That should effectively cut off all feeds from ESEL and Zori would be safe."

Jornash didn't say anything for a moment. He opened several windows examining streams of code. After a minute of checking, he sat back in his chair and shook his head. "I don't think that will work."

Jeremy met Mickey, Bridget, and Natalie's eyes. "Why not?"

"Because," Jornash said as he spun around in his chair. "Only one of you is a real human body. The other three are virtual."

Jeremy gasped. "That can't be true!"

"I'm afraid it is. Natalie's body is the only non-virtual human here. Your three bodies are somewhere else."

Chapter 9

Mickey shook his head. "Can't be. Watch. Exit suit!" Mickey held up his hands and nothing happened. "See? This has to be my real body."

Jornash pointed at a window on a screen. "And yet, here is your virtual feed, active. Everything I have says you are a virtual person."

Bridget wrinkled her brow. "You mean, I'm not really here?"

Jornash shook his head. "Sorry. I wish it wasn't so. I would have gladly taken you up on your offer, but the mask in your pockets are virtual copies as well."

Jeremy ran his fingers through his hair. "If our real bodies are not here, then where? And why can't we exit to them? And when did this switch happen?"

Jornash shrugged. "All good questions with no answers currently. But we do know a few things that would point to some conclusions." He pointed to the virtual feeds flying by. "Each of you three have the ESEL code piggybacked on your feeds. Natalie doesn't. We know that they have to have some physical connection with your masks in order to do that. The logical conclusion is that they have your bodies and masks. How and when, we don't know. But the why is obvious. To take over the virtual world and use it for their own designs."

Jeremy nodded. "That would explain some things, but it's also troubling. If ESEL has our bodies, then once they no longer need us to connect to the virtual world, there's nothing to stop them from killing us."

"True," Mickey said. "But if they want access to our masks, being they only respond to our voices, they aren't likely to kill us anytime soon. I suppose if we cause them enough problems . . ."

Jeremy plopped down in a chair. He bowed his head and stared at the floor. "Now what? They appear to be much further along than we thought if they can do this."

Mickey pointed his finger into the air. "Got it!"

All eyes turned to him.

"Last year, when the group stole our bodies. That's when they had to make the change. They put our real bodies in storage and created virtual copies of ourselves that we thought were the real bodies. We actually freed virtual versions of ourselves. Our real bodies must still be in that complex."

Jornash crossed his arms. "That was a whole year ago. They aren't likely to be in the same location since you know where it is. But it makes sense that they would have made the switch at that time."

Bridget threw her arms up. "You mean, I've been living in a virtual body for a whole year?"

"So it would seem, Sis." Jeremy raised his head. "Seems to me we have two basic options. One, we can go back virtually as superheroes to find out who this ESEL is and see if we can rescue our bodies. Being they will know where we are, that is problematic. Two, we can all return to Earth, hope our bodies aren't in a bad place for this, and I can go into the wormhole as Astro Man and destroy it like I did the one from Similaris to Zori, effectively cutting off the virtual machine to Earth. Based on the situation, I'd recommend option two. What do the rest of you say?"

Jornash raised a hand. "Not too fast. If there is a chance of maintaining our link with Earth, we'd prefer that. You've helped us more than once. Our world would still be under Rillian's rule if not for you three. Who knows what other alien race may want to take over the peaceful Zorians again. Maybe even the SuPutens."

Jeremy met Jornash's eyes. "But we can't guarantee we'll succeed. And I might not be in a position for long to use our superhero abilities, depending on what changes ESEL is making to us. No Astro Man or G Man, and we have nothing to destroy the wormhole."

Jornash smiled. "You've forgotten something. Black Hole."

Jeremy raised his eyebrow. "Black Hole?"

Jornash nodded toward Natalie. "Want to tell him yourself?"

Natalie cleared her throat, having remained silent until now. "It is one of my superheroes that can use gravity like a black hole, can even create them on a small scale."

Jornash patted Natalie on the back. "See? You have a secret weapon ESEL doesn't know about, and can't track. She can work to stop ESEL, and if it fails and they gain too much control of Zori and the virtual world, she can collapse the wormhole."

Natalie's eyes grew big. "Me? Stop ESEL alone? You've got to be kidding."

Mickey put his hand on her arm. "You can do it. You're our only hope." Mickey's eyes widened and he jerked his hand away, glancing at Jeremy. "You have to do it. Zori and me, I mean, we are depending on you."

Bridget hugged Natalie. "Please say you'll do it."

Mickey and Bridget watched Jeremy.

He breathed in deep. "Sounds like the best plan to me. We'll need to get you back to Earth and hide you well, probably with Uncle George. Since we can't run around Earth with you, we'll stay at the station, do what we can from there, and act like everything is normal, except we won't respond to any pleas for help."

Natalie sighed. "I don't have much optimism this will work, but if you want me to give it the old college try, I will."

"The main thing," Jeremy said, "is if I or Mickey can't use our superheroes to collapse the wormhole, you'll have to do it or Jornash here will be forced to shut down the virtual machine and lose most of Zori's culture and progress."

She nodded. "I can't promise anything, but I'll certainly give it everything I've got."

Jornash nodded toward her. "That's all we can ask." He rose from his chair. "Now, how about some seaweed salad before you head back?"

Bridget made a face. "I can eat it. If I have to, I guess."

Everyone smiled as they followed Jornash to the dining room.

————

Jeremy watched the swirling colors of the wormhole through the Eagle VI's view port. It did help to take his mind off of the problems and disappointments. This was only the third time he'd been conscious going through one. It looked a lot like the one they traversed from Similaris to Zori. But it only reminded him that their ultimate goal was to destroy it and lose their link with Zori forever.

Going back to the station, to sit and wait when he thought it would soon be over cast a shadow of darkness over him. Now no visible end was in sight. Their only hope rested with Natalie. Not that he didn't think she could do it, but she wasn't familiar with her powers, based on what Mickey had told him. Nor did she seem mentally the type to figure out what to do quickly. Yet she'd demonstrated plenty of spunk on Similaris. Perhaps she'd come through in the end.

He scanned the room. "Where is Mick? It's his turn to watch things." He'd probably over-slept or something. Jeremy rose from his chair and headed down the hall to Mickey's room. He started to knock on the door, but a girl's voice echoed from within. Sounded like Natalie's. He strained but couldn't make out what they were saying. She giggled and then silence.

He'd made it clear that she should stay away from Mickey. Now she was in his room. It didn't sound like they were just playing a chess game or the like.

Jeremy gritted his teeth and banged hard on the door. "Mick! Get out here!"

Bumping noises echoed from the room, as if someone fell to the floor. Jeremy banged on the door again.

"Okay, okay. I'm coming," Mickey shouted from inside. A few seconds passed before the doors slid open to reveal Mickey's body wearing only shorts. "What's all the commotion?"

Jeremy pushed his way into Mickey's room. "Where is she?"

"Who?"

"You know who. I heard her in here." Jeremy opened Mickey's closet.

He laughed. "Oh, you must have heard me watching a video."

"Of Natalie? Seriously? You have one of those?"

Mickey grabbed a vidplayer by his bed and pressed play. An interview Mickey had done of Natalie describing her homeless experience for a class assignment a half-year ago started playing.

A wave of heat rose to Jeremy's face. "Oh. I'm sorry, Mick. I jumped to conclusions." Jeremy cocked his head to one side. "But why are you watching a video of Natalie?"

Mickey stared at the vid playing. He'd turned the volume down. "Have you seen Natalie in her Black Hole outfit yet?"

Jeremy raised an eyebrow. "No."

"If you had, you'd know why I'm playing a vid of her. Seeing her in that costume is one of the things that set my heart pumping." His face turned a shade of red. "I know how that sounds. But it's true."

"Mick, I understand what you are saying, but you really shouldn't feed the wild animals."

"What?" Mickey squinted an eye at Jeremy.

"You know, at zoos. They have signs saying not to feed the animals. Because if you do, they focus on getting junk from the customers instead of the food they need. You know you can't and shouldn't have Natalie, but you're feeding your desire to do so. It will only make it worse for you."

Mickey chuckled. "You sure know how to analyze the life out of something, Bucko."

"Well, it's true."

Mickey nodded. "I suppose you're right." He shut the vid off and laid it down. "But wait until you see her as Black Hole. Starlight was pretty sizzling as well."

"Mick, I'd prefer you didn't refer to her in that way. She might look pretty sexy, I'll admit, but she's much more than just a body."

Mickey held up a hand. "Oh, I agree. And it is that mind of hers that worries me most."

Jeremy patted Mickey on the shoulder. "You and me both. Now, it's past your time to monitor the ship."

Mickey's eyes widened. "Oh, I totally for-

got! So sorry. I'll get dressed and be right out."
He moved back into his room and shut the
door.

Jeremy started to head down the hall when
Natalie's cabin door opened. She stood in her
pink nightgown, smacking her lips, and wearing her mask. "Oh, hi Jeremy. Can you point
me to the bathroom? I'm so groggy after wak-
ing up that I can't think straight, at least not
until I've had my coffee." She yawned and
stretched her arms.

"Huh, Natalie? Do you always sleep with
your mask on?"

Her eyes flashed open and she put her
hands to her face. "Oh my. Must have forgotten to take it off."

"Why would you have had it on? Did you become virtual?"

She pulled the mask off. Her hair fell down
to her shoulders. "Oh, just practicing. Getting
use to my superheroes. At least the two I
know."

Jeremy smiled. "I've yet to see any of them.
How about this Black Hole Jornash spoke of?"

She grinned. "Sure. She's one of my fa-
vorites so far. But I really need to go to the
bathroom first."

Jeremy swept his arm toward the bathroom.
"Be my guest."

She bowed and then disappeared.

Jeremy glanced at Mickey's door and back
to her. Would Mickey lie to him? Was Natalie
in his room virtually? He hoped not. Not likely.
Surely Mickey wouldn't lie to him. They'd been
friends too long for that kind of thing.

He reentered the control room and checked
on the ship's progress. In a few minutes they
would exit the wormhole and be on the outer
rim of their solar system. They were only
hours away from arriving at the station.

"Hey, handsome."

Jeremy turned around. Natalie stood before him in black boots, gloves, briefs, and halter top, just like the typical female superhero in comics. Sexy and scantily clad. Jeremy smiled. "Sharp."

Her smile shrank into a frown. "Sharp? Seriously?"

Jeremy pointed at her. "Uh, yeah. I mean, like really snappy."

Her jaw dropped open. "Snappy?"

"Though it shows a bit too much skin for my taste."

She gritted her teeth and held her arms stiffly at her side. "Exit suit!" She disappeared.

Jeremy hit himself in the head. He'd done it again. Whatever it was. Sometimes women were so hard to figure out. Not at all predictable like a computer program.

Mickey waltzed into the control room. "How's it going?"

"We're about to exit the wormhole, but I think I'm about to enter a black hole."

Mickey stared at Jeremy as he seated himself. "What?"

Jeremy waved a hand. "Not worth explaining, Mick. I'm going to bed."

"Get some good sleep."

"Thanks." Jeremy left the room, but stopped by Natalie's door. Her sobs reached his ears. He knocked lightly on the door. "Natalie. I'm sorry if I offended you."

"Go away!" she yelled from the other side of the door.

"You did look, really . . . ah, beautiful."

"Leave me alone!"

Jeremy stood at her door for a moment, trying to think of anything else he could say without digging the pit deeper. No ideas arose to fix the situation. He sighed deeply and headed to his own room. He threw on his night clothes and lay in bed.

He dozed off. Fitful dreams played through his mind. He jerked awake as a monster was about to devour him. He could barely open his eyes. He rolled over, twisting his blanket around him, and focused enough to see the time. "Thirty minutes! Is that all?" He let his head drop back to his pillow.

He closed his eyes, but his mind raced to thoughts of ESEL, the fact they likely had his body, and then back to Natalie. He turned to one side, then the other. Thirty more minutes passed and he couldn't shut his mind down to get back to sleep.

Jeremy sat up in his bed and rubbed his eyes. "How dare they make virtual bodies that mimic sleeplessness so accurately." He might as well get up and be there when they arrived at the station. He threw on his shorts and shirt, and headed to the mess hall for some coffee. After popping the straw out and sipping, he headed to the control room.

The doors slid open. Jeremy let the box of coffee float away from his hand. Mickey sat in one of the command chairs. Natalie sat in his lap, facing him. They were deep into a long kiss. Neither of them realized he was there.

The image of her with Mickey burned upon his mind. This couldn't be true, yet there it was happening, right in front of him. How could he deny what he was seeing? Was he dreaming? He wished he was. How? Why?

Natalie broke her kiss with Mickey and squeezed him tightly. The smile on her face said all that needed saying. She opened her eyes. They froze on Jeremy standing in the doorway. Her smile faded into saying the words, "Oh no."

Jeremy breathed in and let the air out slowly. "You could have told me."

Mickey jerked up and swung his head around. He shoved Natalie off him and she sailed through the air and hit a bulkhead. "Oh, Jeremy, I was just . . . just . . . ."

"I know. Showing her the controls. Your controls."

Natalie rubbed the back of her head and pushed herself back to the floor. "Jeremy, I can explain everything."

"No, you don't need to. I can see the explanation well enough. I make you upset, you go find someone else to love on. If that's how it is, you can count me out. I don't want to spend my life worrying every time we have a disagreement whether you're with someone else."

Mickey rose from his chair. "Bucko, don't hold it against her. It's my fault. I should have stopped it."

Jeremy gritted his teeth. "And you, someone I counted as my closest friend. How many years? Since we were five or so? I can't believe you'd lie to me like this."

Mickey bowed his head. "I'm so sorry. I didn't want to hurt you."

"Well, you did. I've had enough of everyone treating me like I'm here for their pleasure and use. Don't expect me to save any of your butts next time you're about to die!"

Bridget entered the room in her nightgown. "What's all the noise? Can't a girl get some sleep around here?"

Natalie knelt before Jeremy and wrapped her arms around his legs. "Please, Jeremy. I blew it big time, but I love you. I don't want to lose you. Please let me make it up to you. Please?"

Mickey pulled his lips tight. "What about me?"

Jeremy yanked his legs from her grasp. "You can have her, Mick. Apparently you were made for each other. Willing to betray your friend for a hot body."

Tears drifted from Natalie into the control

room. Jeremy growled and turned to leave. The control room drifted to black, and then reemerged. The crying had stopped.

"Bucko, look!"

"I'm done looking, Mick."

"No, really, look! Something's happened to the virtual world."

Jeremy turned back around. Mickey's old Mind Game uniform covered his body. Bridget also stood in the control room, dressed in the same white one-piece suit, pen-strips and all. Natalie was gone.

Mickey stared at Jeremy, his eyes wide. "ESEL has rebooted the Mind Game!"

Chapter 10

Jeremy froze, trying to take in Mickey's words through his pity party. "Rebooted? Where are we?"

Mickey checked the control panel. "According to these readings, the same place we appeared when we started the Mind Game the first time. A few hours away from Zori."

Jeremy struggled to focus, but wanted to rip Mickey's head off instead of working with him. The ramifications of what just happened demanded he put that aside, as if he could just turn off everything that happened and his feelings of abandonment. No one really cared for him, save Bridget.

If they could get to the space station, he could leave Mickey behind. Or maybe . . . Jeremy shoved his hand in his pocket. No mask. He raced to his room and entered. All his belongings were missing. He opened drawers and rifled through the items in them, but could not find a mask. He sat on his bed and thought.

"Suit, appear here as Astro Man." Nothing happened. "Exit suit." Still nothing happened. Trapped again, like in the original Mind Game. But surely Rillian wouldn't be back. History couldn't have been erased.

Jeremy shot down the hall and back into the control room. "Mick, see if you can raise Holbreth."

"Good idea." He pressed buttons and an invisible screen popped up over the view port.

Holbreth's office focused in. A Zorian, but not Holbreth, appeared on the screen. "Uh, who is this? Oh, are you Jeremy?"

That was a good sign. The Zorians hadn't lost their history. "Yes. Is Holbreth there? We need to speak to him fast."

"Holbreth? We don't know of anyone by that name."

Mickey glanced at Jeremy.

The Zorian scratched his head. "Do you know how I got here? I was with my family in the city, and suddenly I'm back at the station like I was two of your years ago."

Mickey nodded. "And Holbreth is where he was two years ago. In the underground movement on Zori."

Jeremy put his hand on his forehead. His stomach ached. Too much stress, too much going wrong. He wanted to crawl up into a hole and die. But he never had time for pity parties. They were always cut short.

"You're right, Mick. Somehow, ESEL has reset the virtual world back to the conditions at the start of the Mind Game." Jeremy focused on the Zorian. "Here is what you'll need to do. Send a message to—"

The screen filled with static. When the image returned, a human wearing military style camo and a beret hat stared at them. "Attention, men!" He paused as if waiting for all to comply. Jeremy, Mickey, and Bridget stood straight, though Jeremy guessed the man couldn't see individuals. Appeared to be a public broadcast.

"Today, we will gain the advantage. You've all been given your orders, your area of combat. As members of the Earth Security Enhancement League, we will gain the virtual technology for Earth and its safety. By the authority invested in me as commanding officer of the ESEL invading fleet, I am giving the command to initiate Zori Take Down. I repeat. I command you to initiate Zori Take Down. This is Commander Fisher, signing out."

The static returned for a second before the confused Zorian's face reappeared.

Jeremy leaned forward. "Did you see the vid feed of Commander Fisher just now?"

"No. Just static until you returned."

Jeremy breathed deep. He had to focus. "There is a military group from Earth coming to attack Zori. It is imperative you get all your ships into space, ready to fight. Defend the station, the buildings where your substances are kept, and the lake of the Overlords. We'll be there as soon as we can. Jeremy out." He hit the button to turn the com off.

Mickey shook his head. "They'll be toast up against professionals."

"Not to mention us. Don't you see what's happened?"

"How big do you think their army is?"

Jeremy let his head fall back against the seat. "We forgot the Mind Game helmets. They must have been collecting them. All they had to do was figure out how to override Zori's on-off switch in the programming. They didn't have to create the technology to make virtual bodies. They already had it with the various helmets on Earth."

Mickey slammed his hand down on the control panel. "You mean, all of the 'players' are ESEL soldiers? With instructions to invade Zori?"

"Exactly. Apparently they didn't think that the code feed in our masks would make us part of their fleet. They likely assumed only the Mind Game helmets would do that. But the trap of the Mind Game is now active again. We can't exit the game, and we certainly don't want to invade Zori, nor we can't become any superheroes. All we can do is try to buy some time so hopefully Natalie can get to Earth with her body before the Stuians decide to shut down the virtual machine."

Mickey didn't respond immediately. "Bucko, I'm really sorry—"

"I don't want to hear it right now." Jeremy rose from his chair. "Sis, you keep Mick company. I'm going to do some thinking." Jeremy floated out of the control room and into his room. He crumbled upon his bed and cried.

———

"I don't know why I did it! I'll get help! I'll do anything, Jeremy, just don't leave me!" The control room remained eerily silent. Natalie jerked her head up from her prostrate position. The room was empty. Jeremy, Mickey, and Bridget, all gone.

She scrambled to her feet. "Jeremy! Mickey!" She only heard the humming of the engines and the beeps of the control panel. "Someone? Anyone?" Something had happened. They'd disappeared, leaving her all alone.

She gasped. What if her own body was gone too? She forgot she was virtual as Black Hole. She exited the control room, pulled herself along the hall as fast as she could until she opened her cabin door. She let out a breath. Her body still lay on the bed, mask on. At least she hadn't lost herself.

Or had she? Having Jeremy reject her, to turn so cold on her, forced her to realize what was important. He had loved her for who she was. She had told him by her actions that she'd rather have someone exciting. Sure, he wasn't all that romantic. He'd never gone beyond kissing her. She wanted more movement, a deeper relationship. But in the year and a half of living in the same house with him, he'd kept his distance.

So when Mickey took an interest in her, she found that excitement missing from her relationship with Jeremy. She'd begun to believe her feelings for Mickey were true love. That Jeremy would never love her as more than a sister. But her lies, her deception now rang hollow with the real possibility of losing him. Now the enticing romance with Mickey felt like eating candy. It provided quick energy, but left her empty in the end, forcing her to want more and more. Like a drug. Like those she'd encountered while living on the street. The one good thing she had in her life was Jeremy Goodhue, and now she'd probably lost him.

She stepped up to her sleeping body, drew her hand back, and slapped her face. The pop echoed through the room and her head jolted to the side. A slight tingle emerged through her virtual cheek. "You're nothing but a street bum. Did you really think you'd ever amount to anything?"

She wiped tears from her eyes. The smell of salt hung around her. Nothing she could do now. She was alone. It could be all three had been pulled back to their own bodies. Or who knows what ESEL might have done. It couldn't be that the Sutians had turned off the virtual machine yet, or she'd be floating in space as just a body.

"Buck it up, woman." She stood and blew her nose and wiped her eyes with a tissue. The only way she would win Jeremy back, if it were possible, was to help him now. She had to assume the near worst. Wherever the three of them went, they couldn't use their superheroes or return to her. She only prayed they weren't dead, for real.

Her eyes watered again. What if he was dead? "I don't want to end it like that!" She slapped her virtual face this time. "Get a grip, Natalie. Think. What should I do now?"

She decided to stay virtual. Being a super-hero gave her confidence, and she needed all the confidence she could get. She worked her way back to the control room and checked the journey meter. She'd be arriving at the space station on Titan in thirty minutes. But the only reason they were stopping there was to drop them off. They'd decided she'd take her body to Uncle George's hidden cabin. She might as well go straight there.

She seated herself at the controls. Thankfully, Mickey did spend time between hugs and kisses showing her how to fly this thing. She disengaged the auto pilot and grabbed the wheel. A navigational heads-up display appeared in front of her. She identified Earth, and adjusted course to intersect with its orbit. At least she could fly a ship. That was something.

But, she had a choice to make once she'd left her body at Uncle George's. Did she try to locate Jeremy, Mickey, and Bridget's real bodies and rescue them, or head back to the wormhole to destroy it? While the latter seemed the safest course, if ESEL had their bodies, once the wormhole was shut down and they could no longer use the virtual feeds, they'd kill the three of them and dispose the evidence. She'd need to rescue them before the virtual feed was shut down or she'd never see them again, assuming they were still alive.

"The watch!" It was on Jeremy's virtual body, not his real one. But perhaps if he was still virtual, he could be located. She tapped in the homing signal's frequency. Her and Mickey had tracked Jeremy's location with it before they engaged in their fun. She rubbed her forehead. Some fun this turned out to be. *I've made a royal mess out of it all.*

The signal beacon located him. "Back at Zori?" At least he was still alive. But obviously something big had happened to the virtual world for them to be whisked away involuntarily. She didn't have much time left. If only she knew how much. All she could do was her best. The first task was to hide her body with Uncle George, then find where ESEL held their bodies and rescue them. Then destroy the wormhole.

Saturn floated by her window and disappeared behind her. Loneliness enveloped her. She had been alone on the streets, but this was different. She didn't face saving people's lives then, just finding food for herself. Now she held the fate of worlds in her hands. More importantly, the people she loved most in her life. Somehow, she had to find a way to succeed, or die trying. She couldn't live with the thought of not succeeding.

The last hour to Earth passed quickly as she sat contemplating all that had happened. The task at hand was big. Too big for her. But that's what separated the heroes from those that aren't. Heroes don't give up in the face of overwhelming odds. They keep pushing and moving forward until they are stopped, and then keep pushing. She'd been pushing all her life. Why stop now, despite having lost the love of her life and all she cared about?

As the Moon appeared off in the distance against the big, blue and white ball she called home, she engaged the cloaking. The sphere grew bigger and bigger in the screen. She established orbit, then slowed out of it to descend. Fire engulfed the Eagle's shields, then cleared to reveal cloud tops far below and the blackness of space outlining the curve of the Earth. Millions and billions of people scurried around on the planet below, working, playing, and sleeping. None aware that a half-crazed, virtual woman flying an invisible virtual ship carried her own body back to Earth.

She laughed for the first time since Jeremy discovered the truth. It sounded like something out of a horror movie. *Invasion of the Body Snatchers.* Except she was the body snatcher. She frowned. More like ESEL was the body snatcher, and her task was to snatch them back before it was too late.

The outline of the North American continent grew in her screen. She adjusted reentry to point to Uncle George's hidden cabin. Within minutes she flew over the town close to where he lived and the school she'd been attending with Jeremy the past year and a half. The sun sat low on the western horizon as she flew over his house. She slowed as she approached the mountain on the other side of the valley. She hovered for a moment over the small open field next to his cabin before descending to make sure she'd fit. The legs of the ship settled into the grass.

Natalie cut the power, then stood, her legs wobbly after having been in no gravity for so long. "Exit suit." The control room vanished and she opened her eyes to see the ceiling in her cabin. Hunger attacked her mind. She'd been out several hours, almost a full day. She craved water. She forced herself to her feet and nearly fell, catching the edge of her bed before hitting the floor.

She shook her head. "Yep, the great super-hero is here to save the day! I can barely walk." She pulled herself up and stood on shaky legs. She struggled to put on a shirt and pants.

Once finished, she walked down the hall and opened the hatch. As the log cabin slid into view, so did Uncle George holding a shotgun. He set the gun aside and jogged to the ship, his lips and eyes sharp with fear.

He plodded up the steps of the ship and grabbed her around her waist and put her arm over his shoulders. "Natalie! Has something gone wrong?"

"Uncle, I need water and food. Especially water. Then I'll tell you everything."

He nodded and helped her down the stairs and into his cabin. The hatch of the ship closed. He quickly gave her a cup of water and pulled out bread and peanut butter to make a sandwich.

Natalie guzzled the water down.

"Don't drink it fast. Sip it."

"But I'm terribly thirsty."

"All the more reason to drink it slow. It'll help your thirst faster that way."

She accepted another glass of water and forced herself to take smaller gulps. The water pampered her dry throat.

Uncle George sat at the table and shoved the sandwich on a plate to her. "Now, what's going on? I've been worried sick about you all. Where are the others?"

"Well, it's not that bad . . ." She bit her lip. She was doing it again. Lying to spare people's feelings. If she'd learned one thing, it didn't spare their feelings. It made it worse when they found out you weren't being honest with them. Better that he knows the whole truth. Besides, this time, she didn't mind not being the only one worrying about all this.

"Actually, Uncle, that's not true. It's looking pretty bleak." She launched into the story of what all had happened since they left, her betrayal of Jeremy, and how ESEL did something to the virtual world that took them all three away back to Zori, and how ESEL most likely held their real bodies somewhere on Earth.

"So you see, Uncle. It is up to me to find their bodies before Jornash is forced to shut down the virtual machine. If I don't, ESEL will likely kill them before they can escape, wherever they are. And they'll have no superhero powers to defend themselves with." Natalie hung her head. "Only problem is, I don't feel very super right now. I really let Jeremy down."

Uncle George sat back in his chair. "Yes. You did."

Natalie met his eyes. She expected a hard stare. Instead, compassion poured from his eyes.

"The important thing is you learn from it, make yourself a better person. If Jeremy forgives you and you stay together, he'll have someone he can depend on then. If you don't, he'll have what he had before, and can never learn to trust you. And trust is what holds a relationship together."

"I hope I can do that."

"I know you can."

She gave him a weak smile. "Thank you, Uncle. At least someone believes in me still."

He reached over and covered her hands in his. "Having people believe in you is important. But first you have to believe in yourself. Your confidence comes from within, not from what others think of you."

The warmth of his hands enveloped hers. She breathed deeply. "Have you ever been married or in love?"

He released her hands and sat back. "Never married. But did have a girl in high school."

"What happened to her?"

"Well, she cheated on me. I couldn't forgive her, and she didn't try very hard. It's one of the reasons I decided to live alone up in the mountains for so long. Until Jeremy and Bridget came into my life, and you and Mickey. I've never been so alive in my life."

He leaned closer. "Don't let Jeremy make the same mistake I did. Being a bitter, lonely man is no life for anyone. I wasted years living that lie. Fight for him. Do everything you can to heal yourself and him. Don't allow what happened to be the final chapter on your relationship."

She nodded. "I will." And she knew inside she meant it. No stone left undone. "But what if he never responds?"

Uncle George sighed. "That is his decision. Not one I wish on him, but he very well may go that route. He's in danger right now from more than ESEL. He's in danger from himself."

She rose from the table. "Well, if I don't save Jeremy and the other two from ESEL, he won't have the opportunity to make that decision. So that's the first order of business. We have IV equipment in the Eagle. Can you help me set it up?"

He grinned. "I'm practically and expert at it by now." He stood up.

"I'm thinking my body will be safest hidden in the invisible Eagle. That way I'm not laying around taking up space in your small cabin."

"One problem with that. If the virtual machine does get shut off, you'll drop a few feet to the ground."

She nodded. "Right, but I still think it will be the safest. That way, if you have to escape yourself, you can hide in there, and if there is no other option, you might be able to fly us out of here."

He smacked his lips. "I don't know about that. I can handle a tractor. But not sure about a space ship."

"It's actually pretty easy. I'd suggest you take some time familiarizing yourself with it just in case. If you call out for help, the robot will come and assist you."

He laughed. "You mean that big hunk of walking metal?"

She smiled. "Yep, that's the one." She stepped around the table and grabbed Uncle George into a hug. "Thank you so much. I needed your help more than I realized. I don't feel so alone anymore." She gave him a kiss. This time, on the cheek where it belonged.

He squeezed back. "You're welcome. Now, go and find their bodies. You can do it."

She headed for the door, Uncle George following behind her. "You know, I think you've just about convinced me I can."

Chapter 11

Jeremy entered the control room of the Eagle ship. "How close are we to Zori?"

Mickey swiveled his chair around. "Since you were indisposed, I made an executive decision."

Jeremy rubbed his forehead. This wasn't what he needed now. "I thought we'd decided what we were going to do."

"I know, but I got to thinking—"

"Haven't you done enough thinking lately?"

Mickey swallowed. "What can we do at Zori? One ship against who knows how many ESEL has. And if they've reset to the Mind Game's original settings, they can't track our movements easily since none of the ships can communicate between each other. We're free to go to Su and get reinforcements."

"I had a reason for going to the Zorian space station. We needed to secure Holbreth's office where they would have access to the programming. Plus, I could have programmed in an exit. If ESEL takes that over, it will be much harder to gain access to it. Your executive decision may have costs us big time." Jeremy sat in the other command seat. "What do you think of that? Huh?"

Mickey threw his hands into the air. "Thanks for letting me in on your plans." He turned to stare out at the stars and the growing planet of Su. "Are you ready to talk about it now, so maybe we can start acting like a team instead of two executive decision makers doing their own thing?"

Jeremy gritted his teeth. He hated to admit it, but Mickey was right. As long as this remained between them, they would both be pulling against each other. "Okay. Bottom line, I don't know if I can trust you. You betrayed me."

Mickey dropped his head. "I know. I feel horrible. I allowed her to talk me into it."

"Her to talk you into it? That's not how she portrayed it. She said you wouldn't leave her alone, kept pushing her."

Mickey's eyes tightened. "Really? Strange. That's not how I recall it."

Jeremy leaned back in his chair and crossed his arms. "How do you recall it?"

Mickey cleared his throat. "The part she told you about the kiss when I went to comfort her happened as she said. When she kissed me, it sent me into orbit being my first kiss and all. It scared me though, and I tried to ignore the feelings bubbling up in me from that. Not easy for me. But I was doing it.

"But she came back up to the station with me, at my request. I didn't think she had any feelings for me beyond friendship. So I thought I'd be suffering in silence. When she tried on two of her superheroes, Starlight and Black Hole, I couldn't believe how absolutely beautiful and gorgeous she looked. I mean, I was stunned. Every part of me wanted to grab her."

Jeremy pointed at him. "And that's when you started going after her."

"No. I wanted to, but I didn't. I turned back to focus on the monitors. Then she placed her hand on my shoulder. I think she did notice my reaction and must have liked it. Because she started trying to convince me to kiss her. Granted, in my state she didn't have work at it very hard, but I did tell her I couldn't do it since she and you were together. She convinced me that she thought of her love for you like a brother and sister, and she would deal with you. She convinced me that she wanted a relationship with me and not you. I was fully expecting her to break that news to you at Uncle George's. And, well, you know the rest of the story. I wasn't happy that she was forcing me into keeping secrets from you. I hated it. I've never kept secrets from you."

Jeremy forced himself to relax his grip on his seat. "So why did you keep it a secret?"

"She said you needed to keep your focus on the problems at hand, and telling you the truth would be too much of a distraction. She talked me into waiting until after all this was over. So we were going to tell you, eventually."

"Mick, she was playing you. She told me you instigated everything. She acted like the innocent victim in all this. And she pledged her undying love to me."

Mickey grunted. "I should have known. I feel so stupid."

Jeremy turned back to the controls. "Well, all I've got to say is you can have her. I'm done with women."

"I don't want her. Sure she's hot and makes me go crazy. But I can handle crazy. Done that all my life."

Jeremy couldn't help but chuckle.

"And I meant what I said on Titan before we left. Have you ever known me to hide anything from you before?"

Jeremy met Mickey's eyes. "No. That's why this hurt so much."

"Well, on my part, I'm done with Natalie too. Do what you want, but I'm sure there are other girls out there that can send me into orbit. Until then, Natalie is nothing more than another girl to me. And I won't let her talk me into anything like that again."

Jeremy studied Mickey's eyes. If he could trust anyone, it was Mick. In a lot of ways, he didn't know Natalie that well yet. And what he was learning didn't bode well. Jeremy stuck out a hand. "Mick, I forgive you."

Mickey smiled and took Jeremy's hand. They pulled each other into a hug. Jeremy relaxed. Maybe there was someone he could depend on. They released each other. Mickey wore a big grin.

Jeremy pointed at Su sitting in space. "Okay, we'll see if we can get the SuPutens on our side. They have the most to lose if Zori becomes militarily active again." Jeremy sighed. "I wasn't telling you the whole truth either. I wanted to get to the control room first and install an exit. Get me and Bridget back home, and forget that Zori ever existed. I decided I would run. I didn't want to fight for someone to have them simply use me, again. Saving these people twice should be enough for anyone. It's someone else's turn to be the hero."

Jeremy put a hand on Mickey's shoulder. "But you changed that. Brought back the old Jeremy. Sort of, anyway. Not so sure I can trust Natalie again. I know she was used by the Zorian the first time, but I've just had too much deception from that girl."

Mickey's face turned red. "Thanks, Bucko. That means a lot to me." He hit the com button. "We should be able to contact Su now. Best to get their clearance to land."

Jeremy's world had fallen back into place, at least on some level. Now how best to deal with ESEL and give Natalie time, if she worked on it at all, to free them and Zori from ESEL's plans?

———

Natalie sat in the control room of the Titan space station, suited up as Starlight. With her body safely hidden at Uncle George's mountain cabin, she could focus on locating Jeremy, Mickey, and Bridget's bodies. But where to start? The world was a big place.

She pulled up a window on a terminal and entered the command to bring up Mickey's superheroes. They never had tried to figure out what the last phase shift he'd experienced did to him. She touched the link to bring up new superheroes, and it listed two. The one Holbreth had added and Blue Nova. Captain Subspace was gone. But wasn't Blue Nova an old superhero of Mickey's? Yes, he used it on the last mission they had done together. He was Blue Nova when the phase shift happened. They must have edited it. Instead of inserting a new one, they modified an existing one. The one whose stream Mickey used at the time.

She needed to tell Mickey, before he used it. She froze. He had used Blue Nova once since then, when he moved her and Uncle George to the cabin to escape ESEL. She could send a communication to him, but he wouldn't receive it any sooner than a day. But it was all she had. She accessed the virtual com, but paused. An idea sprung into her mind. If ESEL can locate their virtual bodies based on the feed they carried with them, would it not be possible to trace that feed back to its source? Back to the three bodies?

Problem was, she had no idea how to do that. If Mickey, Jeremy were here, they could do it. Even Bridget could use her find dust as Comet Girl. Though it would be at least two days before she'd hear anything, better to have that option on the back burner than not.

She initiated a com signal to Mickey. She doubted Jeremy would listen to anything she had to say right now. "Mickey, this is Natalie. Two messages I need to give you. No, make that three.

"One, I've determined that the last phase shift you experienced modified Blue Nova. Don't use that superhero again. Using it to save Uncle George and me must have given them the info to take you to Zori.

"Two, I'm working on locating your bodies, but this is not easy. Once possible route is to reverse trace the feed from ESEL piggyback-ing on yours to get source coordinates. You'll probably have to go see Jornash about that.

"Three, I'm very sorry for sucking you into my misguided passions. I do value your friend-ship and hope we can maintain that. But I have to confess that I love Jeremy and if we can work it out, I want to spend my life with him. I hope you will not be too disappointed. I made a mess of it and hope I can eventually straighten it out. I pray you'll be able to for-give me, if not now, eventually.

"Natalie, out." She ended the com signal. Nothing to do there but wait for two days. Meanwhile, she would work on other means to locate their bodies. Now to examine her super-hero list and see if any of them could do anything to aid her. She opened a window and started pouring over the list, reading the abili-ties of each one no matter how stupid they sounded.

––––––––

"The Ascendant will see you now." A Su-Puten opened the door to the room. His insect body, thin trunk, long legs, and praying man-tis-like head, moved to the side. He waved them in.

Jeremy, Mickey, and Bridget entered a room more like a library than an office. The walls were lined with bookcases filled with books and scrolls. A blue carpet ran from the door to the front of a big desk. Behind the desk, carved from a tree trunk, a SuPuten sat robed with blue and purple rings around his sleeves to indicate his rank.

Jeremy bowed. "I am grateful for an audience with your Ascendancy." Mickey and Bridget bowed as well.

The Ascendant stood and pointed at the chairs in front of his desk. "And you honor me with your presence. Sit and let us engage in conversation for the mutual benefit of all."

The three took their seats, and the Ascendant sat after them and focused on Jeremy. "Jeremy Goodhue, it has been a few moons. I pray you are well and your family."

Jeremy glanced at Bridget. He could see the memories of mom and dad resurfacing. "Your Ascendancy, you could not have known, but our parents died in a house fire, caused by Rillian's people. They have been dealt with, but you were not notified. I am sorry for not thinking to make sure Holbreth sent you word of these events."

"I am most saddened to hear this. How long ago?"

"About one and a half years ago. About thirty of your moons, if I understand the time difference correctly. But I'm afraid we are here on more immediate business. There are new aliens who are attacking Zori and want to take over the virtual machine as Rillian almost did. Unfortunately, these aliens are from my planet. Earth."

The Ascendant clicked. "You've been known as the one who brought peace to the region. Now you are bringing war?"

"Not by my desire have they done this. We thought we were being careful. But our continued use of virtual superheroes on Earth alerted them to the power. When Rillian's people attempted to invade Earth, the only thing that repelled them was virtual fighters from the Mind Game. They obviously put all their resources into getting this power. To make a long story short, they succeeded in reinitializing the Mind Game, except instead of an army of video game players, they are soldiers intent on taking over Zori.

"We have a friend . . ." Jeremy resisted the urge to snarl. ". . . on Earth they don't know about, working to stop them there. But we are trapped here again and need to do our best to put up a fight."

The Ascendant waved his thin hands in the air. "And what does this have to do with us?"

Jeremy sat up straighter. "My people are notorious for conquering other lands. Once they control Zori and the virtual machine, they will likely look to Su for their next conquest. If you thought Rillian was hard, you haven't seen anything. Our soldiers are well trained, have fought for years. Unlike the Zorians, they are not afraid to go to war. Some even welcome it."

The Ascendant clicked and rubbed his head with his forearm. "So, you're telling me most humans are not like you?"

Mickey slapped Jeremy on the back. "If they were, Earth would be a safer place. No, trust me. There are not many like Jeremy."

Jeremy glanced at Mickey. "Or like Mick either. But my point is, my people are just now attacking Zori. The Zorians won't hold them off for long. But right now the Earth soldiers are at their most vulnerable. If you join with the Zorians rather than wait for them to attack you, you'll stand a better chance of avoiding a long and costly war like you had with Rillian."

The Ascendant leaned back in his chair. "You make some good points, my friend. Your loyalty to the Zorians and us against your own people is hard to believe. If it were anyone else but you, I'd suspect that you were leading me into a trap."

"I made a promise." Jeremy glanced at Mickey. "I made a promise to the Zorians and the Stuians, to not let my people gain this technology. I knew it would endanger the Zorians if they learned how to use it. Why would I save them from one tyrant to introduce them to another?"

The Ascendant leaned forward. "I believe you, Jeremy Goodhue. I will mobilize a fleet of ships to follow you in the morning."

Jeremy bowed his head. "Your help is greatly appreciated. And the sooner we attack, the better our chances. We're ready to go as soon as you are."

Mickey turned to Jeremy. "An idea. Why don't we go on ahead? Since we look like any other Mind Game player/soldier, we could get in and do something from inside. All the Su-Putens need to know is where to attack."

The Ascendant nodded. "Your friend makes a good point. You get into the station. We'll arrive in eight of your hours to attack. Only one question. How will we discern the Zorian ships from the Earth ones? Aren't they using the same ships?"

Jeremy rubbed his chin. "Yes they are. We'll think of something and let you know. If that is all, we'll be on our way."

The Ascendant stood. "And may all that is good go with you."

The three rose and bowed. After thanking him for his help once more, they returned to their ship and headed for Zori.

Chapter 12

Natalie dropped her head to the control panel and covered it with her arms. "Nothing!" She'd spent the last few hours pouring over her list of superheroes looking for one that had the ability to locate things or people, or enable her to do so. Why didn't she have very many good superheroes? *I mean, Monkey Girl? Who thought of that?*

She lifted her head and scanned through her list again. There was one that might be of help, even if not directly. Yes, there it was. Sensei. A master of martial arts and aerobic abilities, including bending reality. What caught her attention was her ability to read minds by touching someone. It would mean finding someone in ESEL, but if she could, she could perhaps discover where the bodes were kept.

The only link she had to ESEL was that van with "TV 9 News" on it. Mickey recognized it, so they hadn't changed the logo. If she could find that van . . .

But what were the chances? Surely they knew Jeremy, Mickey, and Bridget had been pulled back to Zori. Or did they? What if it were an accident? Maybe, but that still meant the chance of finding that van again was slim.

She snapped her fingers. "The location where they were held last year. They're probably gone, but maybe I could find some clues." She shook her head as she opened up the mission logs. Her solitude already had her talking to herself. She did a search on "kidnapped." When that turned up nothing, she tried "abducted."

Bingo! An entry popped in showing the details of their mission on a plateau in New Mexico on Christmas of last year. She read the coordinates and entered them in. She stood back and called out, "Suit, appear at coordinates as Sensei." The control room dimmed into darkness.

When her sight returned, she stood atop a barren plateau that dropped to a desert several feet in each direction. The wind whipped her hair as she scanned the cloudless sky to determine how much of the day had passed in this location. The sun sank from its zenith. About mid-afternoon. She looked over her body. She wore a black one-piece suit. Strapped to her back lay a case holding an extend-a-pole.

Do I really know martial arts? As soon as she thought it, the knowledge filled her mind. But knowing it and using it were two different things. She spread her legs and squatted, drawing her hands to her side closed into fists. She struck air with her fists in such a rapid succession that her hands blurred. Then she ended with a double-forward kick, rolling into a backflip, and landing on her feet.

She smiled. Reminded her of the abilities she'd had in the Mind Game. Maybe Holbreth had that in mind in giving her this superhero. But she had to try out the other ability. She willed time to slow. A trio of birds flying across the plateau, suddenly froze in mid air. Natalie jogged toward them and stopped in front of them. Their wings moved as if in super slow motion. One beak open, one beak closing, the other shut. *Cool!*

The whole world blinked red. Natalie jerked back and landed on her rear, unsure what it meant. After five seconds of blinking, time snapped back to normal and the flock of birds flew over her. She stayed seated on the ground to get her breath back. Apparently the blinking was to warn her the minute of slow-mo was almost up. According to the description of her powers, she couldn't use that one again for at least thirty seconds.

She hopped to her feet. Time to see if she could find a way into this building. According to the logs, there was an entrance to the underground complex. She sped to the edge of the plateau and scanned the side of the cliff-face. Nothing obvious.

She'd need a different superhero to find this opening and get in. "Suit, appear here as Black Hole." The scene vanished and reappeared. A wind gust gave her goosebumps. Her first reaction was to find what appeared to be a door and blast it out. But if there were people inside, she might hurt them. Likewise, subtly would be best at this point. She wanted to explore and find clues. Not start a war.

She tapped her right forefinger against her cheek. "How can I use gravity to find the entry?" The compound would use refined metals to create buildings and supports within the man-made cave structure. The different metals and vast spaces would affect the gravity field in and around the halls and rooms.

She placed her hands down, palms facing the ground. "Easy now. I don't want to shoot myself into space." She gradually adjusted her own gravity field until her feet floated a few feet over the ground. She leaned in and steadied herself with her hands to fly forward, then sank to the side of the cliff. Using a light gravity beam, she scanned the side of the plateau.

When she found a different pull, she flew in closer and mapped out its size. "This must be the launch bay they escaped out of." She continued scanning the cliff in search of a smaller door. After two hours without luck, she stopped. There must be a different way to get in. Yet, her search had revealed no tire tracks leading to the plateau.

She snapped her fingers. "The plateau!" Why didn't she think about that before? She flew above it and scanned the surface. After thirty minutes, a metallic structure tugged at her gravity beam. She landed by it and walked along its circumference.

She nodded. "A helicopter landing pad made to blend in with the ground. She stood in the middle of it. "Suit, appear here as Starlight."

As Starlight, she shot energy beams into the helipad. The circumference lit up and the helipad creaked before giving way and sinking into the ground. What kind of welcoming committee would she receive? "Suit, appear here as Sensei."

As the pad cleared the top of the chamber, Natalie spotted a group of chains hanging from the ceiling. She scanned the floor below. No one visibly scurried to meet her. Yet, better safe than sorry. Without thinking about it, because if she had she would have sworn there was no way she could make it, she jumped off the platform and sailed through the air until she caught cold steel in her grasp. But instead of hanging on, she swung to the next chain, and the next, dropping downward each time. A moving target would be harder to shoot, if anyone had her in their sites.

She came to the end of the last chain twenty feet above the floor. Swinging into a back flip, she spun four times before extending her legs and arms to land on the floor with her feet and one hand, the other stretched out to block from her crouched position.

She listened. The vast launching bay remained motionless. No sounds other than the buzzing of a housefly off in the distance. She surveyed the area and located the door to the rest of the building. She leaped on top of nearby crates and spun into a forward flip that sent her flying through the air for twenty feet before landing, rebounding back up, and another fifteen feet to land by the door. She could get used to being agile instead of her normal clumsiness. Not to mention this superhero provided clarity of thought as well as knowledge.

She pressed her ear and fingertips to the door. Footsteps. Someone approached. Natalie leaped upward and grabbed a pipe fifteen feet into the air. The door clicked, then opened, and two men in white coats entered the bay.

One of the men pointed at the landing pad. "See, they did come."

"But where are they?" the other man asked.

He shrugged. "Don't know. Maybe birds triggered it. Happened one time before when a flock landed on the pad."

Natalie released her hold on the pipe and went into slow-mo mode as she landed behind them. She reached out her hand to the taller one and touched the back of his neck. Her mind slid into his. They were scientists. The installation had been converted into a laboratory for alien technology once the special unit that captured Jeremy had been shut down. Natalie filled her mind with his knowledge, though much of it didn't make a lot of sense to her.

ESEL! He didn't know who they were, but they were one of the customers of the laboratory. Her vision blinked red. She scurried into the hallway through the open door and leaped up to wedge herself onto the ceiling between the wall and the light fixture.

The men resumed talking at normal speed. They returned from the bay, the door sliding shut and locking behind them. They walked under Natalie but never looked up. After thirty seconds, Natalie dropped back behind them, reengaged slow-mo, and put her hand on the other man's neck.

She entered his mind, and within seconds she hit pay dirt. This man was a secret ESEL agent spying on the laboratory. He didn't have any info on where Jeremy's body had been stored, but did have the location of a regional office for ESEL, hidden in a bar as a front.

The man also knew of technology for extended virtual insertion. A picture emerged from his mind's eye. A cylinder tapered on both ends, transparent all the way around, containing a body floating in a liquid. A breathing apparatus covered the body's nose and mouth, while a tube connected to the belly button supplied liquid and nutrients. She had no doubt that Jeremy, Mickey, and Bridget's bodies lay in such contraptions since they had been virtual for over a year now. She stepped back and released slow-mo.

The two men resumed their progress down the hall. The one she just touched rubbed his neck. "I'm beginning to think everyone has forgotten we're here." They rounded a corner and their voices grew distant.

According to the second man, only two others resided in this underground complex. She doubted she'd find much more information here. She needed to go to regional headquarters and find someone who knew more. First, back to the station to find the coordinates for this office.

"Suit, appear as myself." The control room on Titan replaced the hallway. She headed to a monitor. Making progress felt good. She might be able to pull this off after all. She smiled as she plugged in the name of the bar in a search engine and pulled up the address, and her computers translated it into the coordinate numbers she needed.

She smiled. "This could be fun. Suit, appear at coordinates as Sensei."

———

The space station orbiting Zori peeked over the horizon of the orange planet below. Bridget peered at the wheel-like station rotating slowly in orbit. "Doesn't look like any invasion is going on."

Jeremy hit his head. How could he have missed the obvious? "Of course. The soldiers didn't need to battle their way into the station. What would have been so odd about a group of Eagle's landing on the station? They fly in, position themselves and go where they will. With no leader like Rillian, they would encounter little to no resistance. Chances are they already control Holbreth's office."

Mickey bowed his head. "It's my fault. We should have done what you planned. Now the SuPutens will arrive with no one to fight and the battle already lost."

Jeremy patted Mickey on the back. "I admit, your plan had merit. But now we have two options as I see it. Either we go in and see what they are up to or we head to the Stuians and make sure they are protected. We could redirect the SuPutens there. Plus, maybe they can do something about us being in the Mind Game so we can use our superheroes again."

Mickey nodded. "The second option sounds right to me." He banked the ship to enter Zori's atmosphere.

Jeremy stared at the sinking horizon. "Agreed."

Bridget pulled on Jeremy's arm. "BJ, could Jornash decide to turn off the virtual machine now?"

"That's a distinct possibility if ESEL has

taken programming control of the virtual world. He did say that was the line for him."

She sighed. "Will Natalie be okay?"

Jeremy clenched his teeth. "She's had plenty of time to get her body to Earth. If she dies, it'll be her own fault."

"Is that what you would say if I were there too?"

Jeremy grimaced. "No, Sis. It's just Natalie made me mad before we were separated."

She headed to her seat to belt in. "Hope I never make you that mad."

Jeremy glanced at Mickey. He focused on landing as the atmosphere engulfed the ship in flames. Was he turning into the kind of person he hated? But how could he forget what she had done? To both him and Mickey.

Chapter 13

Natalie appeared in an alley. A cat screeched and shot out from a group of trash cans, causing a lid to fall and echo a clanging racket into the streets. One passerby glanced her way and continued going as if it were a usual occurrence.

Natalie walked to the end of the alley and scanned the street. A business section of town greeted her. Shops of every kind lined the road, and crowds raced to their next destination whether by vehicle or on foot. The smell of gas and diesel exhaust attacked her nose, along with a hint of body odor. She craned her neck to see the sign on the building next to her. It read, "Jack's Hole-In-the-Wall." It matched the business name in the man's head.

Several people stared at her as they walked by. Her one-piece, form fitting, black suit complete with gloves and mask did make her look more like someone about to rob a store than a superhero. One disadvantage in wearing a costume: you don't blend in. But she needed the mind reading power to find out what she needed.

She spotted a clothing store with a trench coat and hats in the display window. That would make her less conspicuous. She didn't have any money, not having pockets, but she'd taken clothing when she lived on the streets a time or two. If you were smart about it, shoplifting was a breeze.

She rubbed her forehead. This is the kind of

thinking that got her in this mess to begin with. Deception to get what she wanted in hopes of not hurting anyone. Not getting caught and having people disappointed in her. She chuckled at the irony that she looked like a robber, and was planning to rob a store. Some superhero she would make.

She recalled in her real body she had some cash she earned before going virtual, and some Christmas money. This would make a good Christmas present for her. She sank back into the alley. "Suit, appear here as myself." After the scene vanished, she checked and now wore the jeans and blouse she'd had on before going virtual. She reached into her back pocket and pulled out the cash she had. More than enough. Only problem, the cash was virtual. It would disappear once she exited the virtual world. It would have to do. She would come back later to give them the real cash.

She stuffed the cash back into her pocket and worked her way through the crowd to the other side of the street and into the shop. She perused the selection of trench coats and landed on a black, leather coat. Then she selected a matching black hat with a short brim, checked out, and returned to the alley. She laid the newly purchased items to the side. "Suit, appear here as Sensei." Once she had changed, she slipped on the coat and donned the hat. She decided she'd look better without the mask, so she pulled it off and stuffed it in a trench coat pocket.

She entered the bar and moved to the counter. The dimly lit room contrasted with the bright sun outside. The bar wasn't busy, being mid-afternoon. Three pockets of people sat with sandwiches and beers, talking among themselves.

"What ya have, lady?"

Natalie met the bartender's eyes. "Just checking out your place here."

He put both hands on the counter. "Lady, you don't even look old enough to be in here. Why don't you move along?"

She lamented that her virtual body didn't look older in this case. "Sure." She dropped into slow-mo mode and placed her hand on one of his. She sank into his mind.

He didn't know anything about where the bodies were, but he knew the doorway into the back room was hidden by a revolving booth, activated by a button under the counter. She released him and reached over and under the counter and found it. She pushed the button and ran to the slowly rotating booth. She crouched under the table against the back wall as snugly as she could muster, then released slow-mo.

The booth swung quickly through the wall and into a narrow hallway. At the end stood a door, guarded by two bulky men. She waited for another thirty seconds to pass to activate slow-mo again, but one of the guards walked toward the booth.

The other guard, holding his hand over his ear called out, "Jack says he didn't know how it was activated. He was talking to some girl in a trench coat, and she suddenly disappeared at the same time the booth rotated on its own."

"All the more reason to check this out." He pulled a gun from under his coat.

He drew close and would see her soon if she didn't do something. She activated slow-mo again, and it started, thankfully. She decided not to bother with these men, unlikely they knew anything. She crawled out, and ran down the hall, opened the door after forcing the lock open with her mind.

Inside, two men sat at desks facing a wall.

A third sat behind a bigger desk facing the other two. If anyone knew anything, it would be him. She placed her hand on his bare arm and reached into his mind. He also didn't know where the bodies lay, but he did know the names of the leadership. Specifically a man called Commander Fisher. And he knew where the primary operations complex was located. On an island in the Pacific. *Of course. Where else?*

The room started flashing red. But she wasn't finished. She needed to check the other two men. She spotted an empty desk. She sped toward it, sank under it, and pulled the chair in to block the view as the scene returned to normal speed.

"Henry," one man at the wall desk called out. "Any news how the invasion of that planet, what's it called, is going?"

The man at the big desk raised his head from his paperwork. "Heard it's a done deal. No resistance at all. They just walked in and took over. The planet's name is Zori."

Natalie realized she needed her mask on. If they saw her and she did anything virtual, they would know it was her and search for her body. Not good.

Henry turned his head her direction. She stopped breathing. He pointed to the desk she sat under. "Did one of you move that chair? I could have sworn it was to the side a moment ago."

"No, boss," they both responded.

The door opened and a guard entered. "Boss, have you noticed anything odd in here?"

Henry sat back in his chair. "Now that you mention it, yeah. It felt, for a fraction of a second, that someone was next to me. But I saw no one. And that chair moved, I'm sure of it."

The guard moved toward the desk.

Natalie reengaged slow-mo and everyone

slowed to a crawl. She hopped out and put the chair back under the desk. Then she slipped her mask out and put it back on. She touched one of the men. He knew less than anyone else from what she could tell by a quick scan of his mind. She put her hand on the other man's neck.

Bingo! This man knew of the bodies. He also spied on regional headquarters for the main one. These guys didn't trust each other. *But where are they?* She continued to search his mind. She was getting close to an answer. The trail of thoughts led the right direction. Her vision flashed red. *No, not yet! I have to find the answer.* Just a few more seconds and she'd have it. *There!* The flashing stopped, and normal speed took over.

The man she was touching jerked back, breaking contact. The guard drew his gun and fired. She started to exit suit, but didn't want to give away that she was virtual. Not yet. She could see the bullets coming at her as if in slow-mo. She slid between them and arched her back to let one pass. Then flipped into the air, landed on the man and wrapped her legs around his neck. Her momentum carried her forward and him backwards as she pulled down to a handspring and flung his body into a wall, leaving a big hole of broken wood.

Henry pulled a gun from his desk while the other two ran at her. She leaped into the air, flipped over their heads, landing with her hands on the desk, and planted her feet onto the rears of each man and shoved them into Henry. They crashed onto the floor behind Henry's desk. Natalie bolted for the door, shutting it behind her. They likely had cameras, so she dived under the booth's table before dropping into slow-mo again. She thought about exiting, but then she'd lose the trench coat she just bought. She kicked through the wall of the booth, knocking a hole big enough to slip through. She sped out of the bar and onto the street, and back into the alley.

As her vision started flashing red, she said, "Suit, appear here as Starlight." When the scene returned, she still had the coat and hat on, but suited up as Starlight underneath. She blasted into the air and headed for Uncle George's cabin. She'd been successful, but only partially. She had located the main base, and the one man who had a memory of three bodies. They'd been put into the cylinders she'd seen from the other man, but they were going to be moved. He didn't know where. Or if he did, she didn't make it far enough to find out.

She sighed as she landed behind Uncle George's house and entered the cloaked Eagle. She shed her trench coat and hat and placed them beside her bed. She'd likely need a good coat when she woke up. At least her body looked peaceful enough. How crazy, to see herself sleeping, and yet, not be sleeping. She wasn't sure she'd ever get used to seeing that.

"Well, girl. Time to find out more at ESEL headquarters." Only problem she had now is they might be on the lookout for her. Why did she feel she was getting in over her head?

––––––––

Jeremy stood behind Jornash as he examined a string of code. Jornash turned around. "We were prepared this time. They have some control over the programming. Minor things. But given what we know of them, they'll find ways to hack into the system. Most of what they've done so far has been through indirect means."

Jeremy nodded. "When I told them my story, I left out about you guys having the final control of the virtual machine. They probably thought taking over the station would give them full control. But even if they can't hack in, they will eventually find you are the source of the wall and come after you."

"The good news is," Jornash said, "that our wall is holding for now. We can delay shutting down the virtual machine."

Mickey held up a hand. "Shush!"

Bridget wrinkled her forehead. "What?"

Mickey waved her back and focused into the distance as if listening to something.

"I don't hear anything."

Mickey wrapped his hand around her mouth and stood still for a few more seconds. Bridget stared at him with a look that said, "Is this really necessary?"

Mickey blinked and focused on Jeremy, releasing Bridget. "I just received a communication." He paused as if not sure to say the rest. "From Natalie."

Jeremy held his breath two seconds before breathing again. "And what did she want?"

"It's not what she wanted. She's warning us. Me specifically. And had a good idea. And she sent me a personal message."

"Personal message?"

"Yes." Mickey swallowed. "I'll tell you later when we're alone." Mickey's eyes watered, but he blinked it back. "But she discovered that the phase shift I experienced last time ended up modifying Blue Nova, and my use of it probably gave them the info to reset the Mind Game."

Jornash's eyes slid open wider, and he returned to his terminal. A window popped open and he examined it for a moment. "She's right. It has been modified."

Mickey rubbed his forehead. "Makes sense. I was Blue Nova when the phase shift happened. The other thing she asked is whether we can do a reverse trace on the ESEL code feed from here to locate our bodies or not? Just like they do to us."

Jornash waved his left hand in the air. "Theoretically possible, but establishing coordinates through a wormhole is very difficult. Doable when the feed ends in the side of the wormhole you're doing the trace from, but on the other side? Near impossible to do a trace from here."

Jeremy sat next to Jornash. "What would she need to do to trace it from that side?"

"She'd need access to the feeds. She would have that at the station itself, since they are piggybacking on its feed and connecting to your feeds from Earth. I could add a program to the station that should do the trick." He opened a window and code flowed into it.

Jeremy said, "Mick, I'll let Natalie know about the program."

Mickey put a hand on Jeremy's shoulder and whispered in his ear, "You may want to hear my personal message first."

Jeremy stared at Mickey. He was open to telling him his personal message from Natalie? On one hand, he seemed to be honest and open with him now. He wasn't keeping secrets. He didn't have to tell him he received a personal note from Natalie. On the other hand, he wanted to not care, not hear it. Forget about her. Why couldn't he do that? "Okay, follow me."

Jeremy turned to Jornash. "We're going to step out in the hall for a moment, Jornash. Bridget, you stay here."

She frowned but said, "Okay."

Mickey followed Jeremy into the hall. Once the door shut, Jeremy turned to Mickey. "Okay, give it to me straight."

Mickey drew a deep breath. "Well, she apologized for sucking me into her passions, as she put it. Said she really did love you, not me, in that way, and asked my forgiveness."

Jeremy faced the transparent wall of the hallway. Fish swam before him, but his mind wasn't on them. He didn't know what to think. Blast it all, he did love her, and that is what made this situation so hard. He couldn't let her keep on going this way. She had to change, and her only motivation to do so might be him. If she was telling Mickey the truth, there would be no more attempts at romance on her part. But if not Mickey, who would it be next? Could he stay with her without worrying about that? Especially if they were to marry?

Jeremy ran his fingers through his hair. "So, are you going to forgive her? In a sense, she was lying to you too. Telling you that you were her true lover when it wasn't true."

Mickey cleared his throat. "Maybe, in time. But I don't think I can trust her again." He laughed. "Not like I ever trusted her much to begin with."

Jeremy smiled. "I agree. I might be able to forgive her. I'll still love her. I just have no idea if I can ever trust her with my heart again." He turned back to Mickey. "Thanks. I'll send her the message."

Mickey nodded and examined Jeremy's expression. He cleared his throat. "Well, guess I'll go see what progress Jornash has made." He left, leaving Jeremy alone in the hallway.

Jeremy watched the fish swim by and the lake bed disappear into the haze of the lake. What did he tell her? He dreaded saying something, yet he didn't want Mickey to do so either. Though he believed Mickey wanted to have nothing more to do with her, he didn't feel comfortable testing that right now. On the other side of the issue, this could be the last chance to say anything to her at all. He had no idea if he'd survive the next day and a half it would take for the message to reach her. He might be dead by the time she received it. He had to say what needed saying with that in mind. And part of him, despite what had happened, wanted to fight for her if there was a chance to redeem the relationship.

He breathed slowly three times to take the edge off his voice. Then he initiated communications to Natalie. "Natalie, this is Jeremy. First, let me tell you what we've done. We can't do the trace from here, but Jornash is changing the space station program on Titan to include a feed tracker. It is set to catch our feeds through the station, and then to our bodies. You should see coordinates on one of the monitors at the station by the time you get this message.

"Second, thank you for catching the change to Mickey's superhero. We currently can't access our superheroes, but that could change, and knowing he can't use that one will prevent ESEL from getting any additional information.

"Third, I wanted to let you know that Mick and I have patched things up. So much so, he shared your message to him with me. So I wanted to convey some things to you since our parting was sudden and, for all I know, by the time you receive this, I'll be dead. As you know, I was greatly saddened by what I saw and from what Mickey told me about how you deceived both of us. I felt betrayed by nearly everyone who is important to me."

Jeremy's voice quivered. He didn't want to get all emotional. But there it was. He needed to do this. "Despite that, I do love you, and I feel I need to say I forgive you. Not because what you did didn't hurt. Not because I feel okay about it all. But because I may not have long to live and I don't want to die feeling bitter toward you. Don't get your hopes up too far. Should we make it through this, I don't know if I'll be able to trust you enough to have a close relationship with you again. I just don't know. But I guess we'll cross that bridge if we get there. Still, I wanted you to know I love you and forgive what you did to me and Mickey. If I don't see you again, I hope you better yourself, find someone special, and have a long and happy relationship with him."

Jeremy tried to think of anything else. "I guess that's it. Take care. Jeremy out." He ended the communication signal and wiped his eyes on his sleeves. That's why this hurt so much. Because he did love her, but he'd lost her. Lost something precious. Could it ever come back? Could it be rebuilt? Or would he live in fear of a repeat if he married her?

The door slid open and Mickey burst into the hall. "Bucko! Some scout patrols have been seen over the lake. They're coming!"

Chapter 14

Better to go right away than to give them time to prepare. Natalie, as Starlight, opened the Eagle's hatch, flashed out, and arrived at the Pacific Island coordinates in less than a minute, only because she took a wrong turn at Hawaii. She stopped and hovered eight thousand feet over the island to check the compound's layout. She lowered herself to five thousand feet to get a better look. Starlight chose a spot, then flew toward it with all her speed. At near light speed, she arrived in less than a second. She landed between two buildings.

I wonder how inertia is overcome so easily, dropping from light speed to zero in one hundredth of a second? But this was a virtual body, after all. It could be programmed to violate all sorts of physical laws. Which only made the point, who had the bright idea to limit Sensei with just one minute of slow-mo time?

But it was time to ditch the silver outfit that shown like a beacon in the night for a more covert one. "Suit, appear here as Sensei." The moonlight casting eerie shadows over the grounds vanished and then reappeared. Now, where to start. Any guard should know the layout of the grounds here. How else would they know what they are guarding?

She moved to the corner of the building and waited in the shadows. After a minute, two men in uniform marched by. When they passed her, she slipped into slow-mo and touched one of their necks. She quickly found a building containing a slew of the cylinders with bodies inside. Jeremy had to be in one of them. But this guard didn't know specifically about them.

She released him, dropped back into the shadows, and allowed normal speed to resume. She located the building in her mind based on the guard's memories. Once a minute had passed, Natalie reentered slow-mo and ran for the building. Unfortunately, two men were exiting the door, barely creeping along. She dived and rolled between their feet, knocking one a half-step wider in the process. Sensei rolled to her feet and bolted for the next door. She yanked, it flung open, and Natalie fled down the hallway, slipping between people as she did. She reached the door to the main virtual insertion chamber, but it was shut, locked, and requiring a retinal scan.

The hallway started flashing red. "Oh bother." She leaped to the high ceiling and wedged herself into the corner. The people started walking at normal speed and conversation resumed. If anyone looked up, she'd be in trouble. The door to the room opened. She resumed slow-mo mode and dropped to the floor. She squeezed between the man's legs and into the room. To her right lay a control room set up. Before her sat rows and rows of the long-term virtual insertion cylinders. She needed to get info on which ones contained Jeremy, Mickey, and Bridget. She could spend hours in here looking for them.

Figuring one of the people in the control room likely knew, she hurried into the room and placed her hand on the head of one who appeared to be in command. She searched his mind. He was thinking of a girlfriend he would see after he was released from duty. She pushed past those, feeling a little jealous, and reached further in. There, a thought about Jeremy. She followed the trail. She gasped. *They're not here! They're in orbit!* The room flashed red. *But where in orbit?* She searched further. No idea. The person only knew they were in orbit. Natalie checked the control panel in front of her. Readings for three life signs displayed with additional information. She took a mental picture of the screen.

The room returned to normal time. She didn't care now. She had what she needed. "Exit suit." She didn't disappear. The people in the room leaped to their feet and headed toward her. She sped toward the door. A man entered and blocked the door. He held a gun with a thick cord dragging behind him. He fired. Electrical bolts arced from its nozzle. Natalie tried to dodge them, but there were too many threads, too thick, and too fast. They covered her body.

No! I have to save them before ESEL . . . She blacked out.

———

Jeremy followed Mickey into the code room. Jornash hovered over his monitor. Jeremy peered over Jornash's shoulder. "Do you think the scout picked up anything? We hid the ship as best we could. Unfortunately, the version of the Eagle for the Mind Game didn't include cloaking abilities."

"Hard to say. They did two passes. We're deep enough in the lake bed it would take a particular type of scan to pick us up. Depending on what scan they used, we may have been discovered."

Mickey nodded. "We'll have to assume they saw something. They'll likely send more scouts, some on the ground, maybe with scuba gear."

"Possibly." Jornash spun around. "But I do

have some good news. I've found the exit command for the Mind Game. They apparently put one of their own in so they could leave when they wished. You simply say, 'Mind Game, exit ESEL Zori Takedown mission.'"

Bridget clapped her hands. "You mean we can go home?"

Jeremy held up a hand. "Hold on, Sis. It may not be so easy."

"Truer than you know. You see, I don't think they know you three have been sucked into the Mind Game. For the same reason it's very hard for us to find coordinates in your world from here, those on Earth are not able to detect your location by virtual feed while you are here. Not having planned for you to be here, they can no longer track you. And if someone on Earth does notice you've disappeared, it will take more than an Earth day to get a message to the force here.

"What they didn't plan on is when your fake real bodies were drawn into the reset Mind Game, it reset what an exit would do. In short, if you take this exit, it should return you to your real bodies."

Mickey frowned. "But if we left, you'd be defenseless, at least until the SuPutens arrived. Problem is, this time they are not facing reluctant and untrained Zorians, but skilled soldiers. The only advantage I have over them is I've played a lot more video games than most of them, and this is what the Mind Game is. One big video game."

Jeremy nodded. "By the time we reappeared on Earth, wherever that might be, you might have been taken over. You'd have to shut down the virtual feed before we could destroy the wormhole."

Jornash grinned. "You must think us a backward race to not have planned proper defenses. We'll last longer than you think.

Mickey, you stumbled upon the defense against virtual people when Similiaris attempted to invade Earth. Do you remember?"

Mickey scratched his head. "My gravity beam?"

"Exactly. The virtual machine runs from the planet's gravity field. Disrupt that into a negative field, and the virtual body falls apart. When we engage it, the water's surface acts as a negative gravity field shield. Any virtual ray, ship, or soldier who attempts to go through it, disappears into thin air."

Jeremy raised his eyebrow. "How come you've never told us about this before?"

Jornash smiled. "Seriously? Would you tell all your anti-virtual secrets to virtual people?"

Jeremy hit his forehead with his palm. "I know. I'm too trusting sometimes. I'm learning you can't operate like that."

Jornash shook his head. "Has nothing to do with trust, my friend. Everything to do with prudence. Now, I suggest you three return to Earth and see if you can shut down the wormhole before I'm forced to shut down the virtual world."

Jeremy nodded. "But, let's all go in five minute increments. I'll go first. That way if need be, I can help each of you when you arrive."

Bridget hugged Jeremy. "I hope we're okay."

Mickey patted Jeremy on the back. "Don't forget. Our bodies have been lying idle for over a year now. They'll be weak."

"Mick's right. We should be wearing our masks. So as soon as you awake, become a superhero so you can carry your body out." Jeremy caught each eye. "Are you ready?"

They both nodded their heads. Jeremy turned to Jornash. "Thanks for everything. I guess one way or another, this is the last time we'll be on Zori."

"No, thank you." Jornash put a hand on Jeremy's arm. "You've taught us what real friendship looks like. May peace follow you."

Jeremy smiled. Despite his eagerness to end this virtual life and be normal again, he would miss his Zorian friends. "One last thing I need to do." He initiated a com signal connection. "Natalie, this is Jeremy again. We've found a way to come home. We'll be returning to our real bodies. Hope to see you soon. Jeremy out." He ended the signal.

Mickey and Bridget stared at him. Mickey grinned.

"What?"

Bridget cocked her head. "Are you no longer angry at Natalie?"

Jeremy sighed. "Not angry, just disappointed and sad." Jeremy met Mickey's eyes. "As you say, Mick?" He waved a palm toward his friend.

Mick smiled. "Let's do this."

Jeremy grinned. "Mind Game, exit ESEL Invade Zori mission." He sank into darkness.

———

Natalie awoke in her jeans. Was she back in the Eagle? She focused her eyes. No, this was not the Eagle. Surely they didn't find her body. She said softly, "Exit suit." Nothing happened. This may not be her real body. It could be one of those virtual dampening fields Jeremy experienced with the Similarians. After all, she hadn't been able to exit the control room of the compound. And the stun ray the soldier shot at her, very similar to what she recalled the SuPutens using in the Mind Game.

Just to make sure, however . . . "Suit, appear here as Black Hole." Still nothing happened. She rose to her feet and walked the perimeter of the room. Her memory returned to events in the control room. She covered her face with her hand. Jeremy, Mickey, and Bridget lay in a satellite orbiting Earth. On top of that, the last memory she pulled from the man before she broke contact was that the satellite was rigged with atomic explosives set to detonate if the satellite or the cylinders were opened. And no provisions had been made to disable it. As soon as one of them returned and opened their cylinder, all three of them would be killed.

Here she was, unable to do anything about it or warn them. She had to find some way to break out of here.

A screen lit up against one wall. An older man, thin faced, short hair, wearing a beret, appeared on the screen. "Good morning, Miss Shinhaw."

He knew who she was. Not a good sign.

"I suppose you are wondering why your virtual superpowers are inaccessible to you now?"

"Not really." No sense letting him know she had an inkling of how it worked.

"That is good, because we wouldn't tell you anyway. But I do have a few questions for you. Where is your body?"

She repressed a smile. Good, he didn't know where her body lay. She was still virtual. "You're so all knowing. Why don't you tell me?"

He smirked. "I had a feeling you'd be less than cooperative. As you may have guessed by now, I have the bodies of your three friends. They are surrounded by explosives. All I need to do to end their little lives is push this button." The camera panned down to show his finger poised over a big, red button.

Why was it always a big, red button?

The camera panned back to the man's face. "Practically speaking, I no longer need them. We have taken over Zori. It will only be a matter of time before we control the virtual machine. They have played their part in my scheme well enough. The question is, are you finished with them? Will you answer my questions or let them die?"

If what he said was true, he'd likely kill them anyway. If not now, soon. There would be no reason to risk Uncle George's life and her body for promises that would likely prove false anyway. "You're bluffing."

"Maybe. Maybe not. Are you willing to gamble your friends' lives on that assumption?" The camera moved back to the red button. His finger hovering over it.

Once they had gained access to Zori's world programming, they wouldn't risk three superheroes messing it up for them. They'd get rid of them. If they were still alive, ESEL still needed them to link to the virtual world.

Natalie smiled. "I'm a gambling type of woman. You'd best go ahead and push that button."

The man's voice echoed from above the camera with an irritated edge. "You've left me no choice, Miss Shinhaw. The button plunged down and a click sounded. She heard an explosion rock the building. The camera returned to the man's face. "I hope you are happy that you've killed your friends." The screen went blank.

That confirmed her suspicions. He thought hearing an explosion nearby would convince her. He didn't know she knew they were in orbit. Not here on the island. He had been bluffing. Thankfully. She leaned against a wall. Now what?

Chapter 15

Most of a day had passed. The man came on occasionally to grill Natalie, and offer some other bluff. One time it was killing Uncle George. Another, Mickey's parents. Always ending with an explosion off in the distance. By now she didn't believe a word he said. When he showed her a live human, then maybe she'd think twice about it. He was running out of loved ones to kill, however. He must know this wasn't working on her.

She stood and examined the room. The walls were bowed, like the room on the Similarian space ship where she and Jeremy had been trapped. It also had the same covered structure about three feet in diameter dropping about four feet down from the center of the ceiling. But she noticed on this one, a small hook rested in the center of the protruding section. The protrusion must be the projector of the virtual dampening field. Did the field have dead spots?

She slowly followed the perimeter of the room, mumbling to herself the whole time, "Exit suit." If she hit a dead pocket, she'd be out of here. After two hours, she had worked her way to the center, but no luck. She stared at the protrusion. If there was a dead field in the room, it would be directly under the projectors. But how to get up there?

The lights dimmed until it appeared to be dusk. Must be her clue to get some sleep. She lay on the floor against a wall and stared at the projectors. An idea formed in her mind. She unbuckled her belt and slid it off her pants, then laid it to the side. She unzipped her pants and pulled them down, and in turn, threw them on top of the belt. Likewise, she slid her blouse over her head and threw it beside her pants. Then she unbuckled her bra and pulled it off. That always felt so good, like being freed from prison.

She snuggled onto the floor as best she could, using the pile of clothing for a pillow. The air gave her bare skin a chill, but she had to do this in hopes her theory was correct. She closed her eyes and pretended to go to sleep. She waited for what she judged to be an hour, in hopes whoever watched her "striptease" show had moved onto other things like football, a movie, or a good book. Then she slowly took one of her pants legs and tied it into a knot with one end of her bra. She tied the other end of the bra to her belt. The blouse would be too weak for this task, so she left it on the floor.

She lay for another thirty minutes to make sure no one had grown suspicious with her movement. No reaction. She pulled the tied clothing to her and rose from the floor. She cast the end of the belt buckle toward where she remembered seeing the hook. After five tries, it caught. She tugged on the makeshift rope and began climbing, all the while saying, "Exit suit," over and over again.

The lights kicked into full brightness, so much it blinded her. She kept climbing and saying the words. Speakers began blaring a hard rock song with grinding electric guitar. She yelled at the top of her lungs, "Exit suit!" She reached the top, bumping her head against the bottom of the projectors. The door to the room flung open and men pointed guns at her. The music stopped.

"Get down to the ground. Now."

"Exit suit."

Bullets ripped into her chest; the room vanished.

———

Natalie jerked upright. She lay in the Eagle. She'd returned to her body. She patted her stomach through her blouse. No holes or blood. How long had she been trapped in that room? She disconnected the IV and wobbled her way into the mess hall. Uncle George had stashed some real food for her. She thanked him as she opened up and bit down on a sandwich. She popped open a soda and enjoyed every drop.

She sat at the table while enjoying her meal. Somewhere among the various satellites circling Earth flew one with all three bodies in it. While that narrowed it down a good bit, it could take forever to go through all the junk up there. And how would she know she'd found it. And if she found it, how would she bypass the explosives? She could potentially shield them as Starlight, but she didn't know if her shielding would stand up to a nuclear explosion, and she'd have to get inside for it to work.

While she could appear virtually inside of it, that might be a tall order for an object moving so fast. One set of Earth coordinates would only be good for a second or less. The virtual machine was good at putting a person in a habitable place, otherwise they would have been embedded in buildings or trees by now. But if she missed, it could set off the explosives. Too big a risk.

Well, one task at a time. First order of business was to find them. Now that ESEL knew another virtual superhero was on the loose, they would respond appropriately. At least they had no idea she knew Jeremy, Mickey, and Bridget were in orbit, so they'd probably leave them there.

She threw her trash away and headed for her room. Time to return to the station and plan her next move. She lay down, reconnected the IV, and said, "Appear as Black Hole." The room vanished into blackness and the control room of the Titan station filled her vision. A high pitched, beeping noise echoed through the room. She sat in front of a monitor displaying a window. In the window were a set of continually changing coordinates. But where did they go?

A communication signal registered. She acknowledged it and sat back to listen. It was Jeremy! Of all people. She sat up straighter. He thanked her for warning Mickey about Blue Nova. Her eyes grew wide as he explained that Jornash had used the station to put a trace on their feeds. The coordinates on the monitor indicated their real bodies' locations! She gave a victory pump. "Yes!"

Then her joy quieted as Jeremy gave her his personal message. He forgave her, but wasn't sure about the relationship. She couldn't keep the tears back as he signed off. She flopped onto the control panel sobbing. Would she see him again? And if so, would he ever trust her again? She lifted her head. What did she expect? The boy had been deceived by her, sort of, in the Mind Game. He thought for a good while that she deceived him when they were captured by the Similarians. And now this affair with Mickey.

She wiped her eyes. She'd said it. That's what it was. An affair. She had been Jeremy's girlfriend. She ruined it. What did she expect would happen? She knew it would break his heart, but she refused to think about him, only what she wanted. She deserved whatever the consequences were.

But Jeremy didn't deserve it. He didn't deserve to die. And she would do all she could to make sure that didn't happen, whether she remained his girlfriend or not. She entered the coordinates, but adjusted them slightly to make sure she didn't get too close.

"Suit, appear at—"

Another communication signal beeped in her head. She acknowledged it. Jeremy's excited voice announced they'd found a way to escape, and would be returning to their real bodies. He said, "See you soon," as if he was excited at the prospect. That sounded encouraging.

She gasped and hit her forehead with her palm. "No, no! If they open one of those cylinders . . ." She had to act fast. "Suit, appear at coordinates as Black Hole." The control room disappeared.

––––––––

Jeremy jerked as he came to. His body floated in a liquid. He breathed through a hose and a tube connected to his belly button. The thought made him sick. He shouted out as well as he could with a mouthpiece stuffed in him, "Suit, appear here as Astro Man." The fuzzy underwater world vanished and he appeared in a short hallway. Three transparent cylinders, tapered at the ends to a point, lay on raised beds over the floor. His body, Mickey's body, and Bridget's body were dressed in swim suits. The cylinders were filled with a liquid, and the hose connected to each belly button. Fancy IV, he guessed.

He was floating as if in space. But where in space? He didn't know. No windows provided an outside view. He'd have to reappear at coordinates that would be outside this room. But how far did he need to go? Was this room part of a space station, or a single ship? Another thing, the room lacked a door. However they had sealed them in, they didn't intend to open it again.

Jeremy examined the cylinder containing his body. Locking clamps rested evenly along the vertical circumference. Judging by a diagram on a wall-mounted control panel, flipping two switches would cause the cylinder to drain and open. Then he could get his body out. Jeremy reached for the levers, but paused. "Why would they go to all the trouble to put us in space? It would have been far more economical to hide us on or below ground."

Jeremy examined the cylinder seals until he found sensors on both the top and bottom. *Why would they want us in space, in a sealed container, unless they wanted to ensure any attempt to escape or break out would result in death?* The possibility it was rigged with explosives was high. He scanned the room and found an air pressure display. Likely any loss of pressure would set it off too. So blasting a hole in the wall wasn't an option. Not to mention if he shot a hole in the wrong spot, he could set off the explosion.

He heard banging on one of the cylinders. He spun around to see Bridget hitting the inside wall, her eyes wide in panic. He rushed to her and yelled, "Virtual, go virtual! Remember?"

She nodded and closed her eyes. Comet Girl appeared in the hallway. She stared at her body in the contraption. "Where are we?"

"Best I can figure is in space, and I suspect this room is rigged to explode if anything is opened. They never intended for us to leave this room alive."

"You mean, we can't get our bodies out?"

Jeremy put his hand on his helmet. "I

haven't figured out how yet. Maybe Mick can help when he gets here."

"Jeremy?" Natalie's voice echoed over the com.

"Natalie!" Despite all that happened, hearing her again excited him.

"Whatever you do, don't open the cylinders containing your bodies. It will explode. Nuclear."

Great. "I guessed as much. Any idea on how to get us out of here? I'm running through our abilities and can't think of anything. And I'm sure we need to get out of here quickly. As soon as they see they've lost our feeds, they're likely to set this off."

She didn't say anything for a few seconds. "No, not any solid ideas. You're enclosed in a satellite orbiting Earth."

"What about mushy ideas?"

"Well . . . I do have an idea, but it is a long shot. Have no idea if I can pull it off."

"We don't have much time left. What is it?"

"You intentionally set it off. You can create a shield, maybe Mickey can use G Man to help. If I do it right, I should be able to use the gravity forces of Black Hole to pull the explosion one way while pulling your bodies in the shield out the other. Like pulling a pit out of an olive."

"What will happen to Earth if we create a gravity well next to it?"

"I don't know." She paused. "That's the mushy part. I'd have to make it strong enough to suck the explosion in, but not so much it begins to pull apart Earth."

"Could you tow it away from Earth?"

"I have no idea if I could do it without it exploding."

"Bucko!" Mickey placed a hand on Jeremy's shoulder. "What's the scoop?"

Bridget pointed at their bodies. "We're going to die is the scoop."

Jeremy nodded. "It doesn't look good, Mick."

"Since when does it ever look good?"

"No, I mean, like our bodies are trapped in a capsule orbiting Earth loaded with nuclear explosives that could be activated at any time or by opening anything."

Mickey examined the hallway. "Oh. I see."

Latches busted open as air pressure kicked the locks to the cylinders open. Each of the three cylinder doors popped open, and the liquid drained onto the floor. A digital readout on the far end of the hallway lit up and a woman's voice counted, "30, 29, 28, 27 . . ."

"Natalie, the cylinders just opened on their own. A countdown started from thirty seconds."

"Arg! They must have noticed your feeds no longer existed. Blow a hole and get out."

"No, that would set off the explosion when we're not ready. Move us away from Earth as far as you're able. I'll tell you when to stop. You're mushy plan is on. It's all we've got."

Mickey moved into Jeremy's field of vision. "What mushy plan?"

"No time to explain. Everyone, grab your bodies and gather in the center of the hallway. As quick as possible."

"20, 19, 18 . . ."

Jeremy disconnected the tube to his belly button and pulled off the electrodes. He dragged his body to the middle of the floor. He checked Bridget's progress. She still struggled to get the tube off.

"14, 13, 12 . . ."

Jeremy grabbed the tube from Bridget. "Pull off those electrodes." He twisted, but it was stuck. He grabbed firmly and yanked it counter clockwise. It broke free, though she bled where it connected to her skin.

"8, 6, 5 . . ."

As Jeremy pulled Bridget's body over with his, he said, "Natalie, stop and get ready!"

"4, 3 . . ."

"Mickey, put up the strongest gravity shield you have. Everyone hold their bodies."

"2 . . ."

Mickey threw up a hand; Jeremy pulled the gun from his holster and fired the force field ray.

"1 . . ."

"Now, Natalie. Now!" Jeremy covered Bridget as well as he could, though the virtual bodies wouldn't matter.

The walls around them fractured into lines of fire and irradiated inward. White brightness flooded his vision, Jeremy slammed his eyes shut. The intense heat reached its fingers through his and Mickey's shields. But as suddenly as it moved forward, it pulled back. The hallway fell away from them as if peeling a banana. The gun in his hand burned him, but he held on, keeping the trigger pulled. The debris and white fire fell away from them to reveal the darkness of space. Black Hole floated a few feet away.

"You did it, Natalie!"

Mickey cleared his throat. "It may not be over yet, Bucko." He pointed at their bodies. Their skin was red. "We need to get us to a hospital."

Jeremy shook his head. "Natalie, get us to Earth before we run out of air. Go to a hospital in Chicago. That's your neck of the woods."

"We're on the way." She shot a ray at the group sitting in Astro Man's shields and towed them toward Earth.

Mickey looked over his shoulder. "Smart."

"What?"

"Natalie used the Sun's gravity to create the black hole that sucked the explosion away from us."

Jeremy smiled. "Yes. Perfect. The Sun can handle a nuclear explosion and a mini-black hole, temporary as it was."

Bridget asked, "Should we exit virtual yet?"

Jeremy glanced at Bridget's red body. "Not until you have to. I'm sure you're in pain."

Within a minute, they flew over Chicago. Natalie landed them outside a hospital, in the grass not far from the Emergency Room. Jeremy released the force field and holstered his gun.

Jeremy stood before Natalie. He had to admit, in the night moonlight as Black Hole, she did look pretty hot. "We won't be able to use our superheroes for a while. It is up to you to collapse the worm hole. As Black Hole, that should be a snap."

She nodded. "Consider it done." She stared at the ground. "Jeremy?"

"Yes?"

"Did you mean it when you said you wanted to see me again?"

He swallowed. "Yes. But we can talk more if we survive whatever radiation leaked through our shields. First things first. Stop ESEL. They think we're dead now, so they won't be looking for us."

"I understand." She stepped away. "Suit, appear here as Starlight." Her form vanished, then reappeared. "Speed of light and all." She winked and smiled, then flew into the air so fast it seemed she disappeared.

"Okay guys. This is the hard part. Expect pain. I'll go get the medical folk while you exit back into your bodies."

They both nodded.

Jeremy said, "Suit, appear here as myself." When he reappeared, he ran into the emergency room. "Burn victims lying on the ground outside! Hurry!"

Two nurses jumped from their seats and followed Jeremy to the bodies lying outside. One said to the other, "Quick, get the doctor and beds." She knelt to start checking their status.

Jeremy said under his breath, "Exit suit." When he returned, burning pain shot over his body. He jerked up and flung his eyes open.

"Calm down, sir. We're taking care of you." She turned her head. "Sir, can you tell me . . ." She scanned the area. "Where did he go?" She shook her head as the sound of cart wheels wobbling on pavement pierced through angry pain.

Chapter 16

Natalie sat in the Eagle VII's control room, watching the depths of space for the wormhole. She'd been flying for nearly four hours from Titan at near the speed of light. She could have flown here in the same amount of time as Starlight, but she needed the navigational help of the ship. Space was a big place. Easy to get lost.

Jeremy's words when she left gave her a glimmer of hope. He'd not said there was hope. She really couldn't expect him to say as much either. But the fact he was willing to talk with her provided some optimism that they could work it out. "I've got to work on myself. Do whatever it takes to make sure it never happens again."

The wormhole's opening caught her eye. She could see the beginnings of the hole snaking off into space. Soon this would be over. She didn't even need to go into the wormhole, just sit on its edge and fire her black hole power into the gulf. The collapse should produce a cascade effect all the way to Zori's system.

The opening grew bigger and bigger. Knowing she was still the same distance as Mercury from the Sun, she judged it to be at least the size of two Earths. She'd arrive there in minutes. Which ticked by agonizingly slow. She wanted to finish this and get back to Jeremy. In a few minutes, she should be falling onto the ground behind Uncle George's cabin.

She frowned. She hadn't thought of that. Not having any superpowers or virtual space ships once this deed was done, she'd actually have to fly in a plane to Chicago. It would still take hours, maybe most of a day, to get there. She sighed. Nothing could be done about that. She'd have to suffer.

"Only another minute and I'll stop. That should be close enough." She straightened herself in the chair and watched the journey meter count down the distance to the wormhole.

Darkness swept over her. When light reappeared, she lay on her bed in the Eagle VI, dressed as herself. An IV dripped fluid into her. "Something kicked me out of virtual!" She grunted as she slammed her hand on the side of the bed. She so much wanted this to be over.

She lay her head on the pillow. "Suit, appear as Black Hole." She reappeared in the Titan Control Room. She checked the launching bay—the Eagle VII was sitting in it. She entered it and checked its logs. Yes, it did show she'd traveled to about a minute from the wormhole, but then it stopped. She noted the coordinates and entered them into her suit.

"Suit, appear at coordinates as Black Hole." The control room disappeared to be replaced by the swirling colors of the wormhole in the distance. Natalie put her hand out and slowly moved forward. In a few seconds, her hand disappeared. She stopped and withdrew her hand. It returned to the end of her arm.

A virtual dampening field around the entrance to the wormhole. Just great. It must allow the virtual feed to go through, or she wouldn't be here. She backed up and extended both hands forward. Green rays erupted from her palms and blasted gravitational energy against the field. It wavered, but the rays disappeared at the edge of the field. She continued, adjusting the gravity from positive to negative, but nothing happened. After five minutes of it, she stopped.

Maybe I can find a hole in the field or go around it. She flew one direction, giving short blasts of her rays to "sound" out the edge of the field. Gradually, over an hour's time, the edge of the field moved further away from her. A positive sign. She flew in closer and continued sounding the edge as she flew. After another hour, the blasts had grown further away from her again.

She stopped and evaluated her position in relation to the wormhole. The edge of the field circled the opening. The field was a sphere. And based on the size of it, it would take days to check every possible spot for a weak link.

She grunted and pointed both palms at the field, and drew close. She formed two little black holes from her hands. The field flexed, but the black holes couldn't break them. *Stupid ESEL!* She gave a final gravity ray blast with all her might. It vanished into the field without so much as a whimper.

A glint of distant sunlight met her eyes. She gazed harder and realized four satellites sat just behind the wormhole's entrance. The dampening field projectors. So no chance of taking them out either.

Now what? None of my powers can do anything to get past this. What am I missing? She mulled options over in her mind, trying to be creative, but no ideas emerged. *I've failed. Jeremy will likely not even talk to me now. ESEL probably figured Jeremy, Mickey, and Bridget are dead. The only virtual threat to them is me. And they may be right for all I know. And if so, it is only a matter of time be-*

fore they find my body. I can only hide for so long.

A communication signal beeped in her mental ear. She quickly acknowledged it. "To Jeremy, Mickey, Bridget, and Natalie from Jornash. I waited too long. I did succeed in locking down the virtual machine access, but they will eventually break into it and learn its secrets. The only hope for Zori, for you, is to collapse the wormhole before they can hack into it. I pray you will succeed where we have failed. I . . . have to go. Someone is coming. Jornash out."

Natalie stared at the rainbow of colors swirling inside the wormhole. ESEL had won. They had successfully taken over Zori, prevented her from destroying the wormhole, and put Jeremy, Mickey, and Bridget out of commission, maybe for good. She was the sole hope to stopping this, and right now, she didn't feel anymore able to do a thing about it than a janitor at the hospital.

She bowed her head. "Exit suit." In a flash of darkness, she stared at the ceiling of her cabin through watering eyes. She covered her face. Now what? She could go into ESEL's headquarters, rays a blazin'. But she'd only be a mosquito for them to swat. She had to hand it to them, they had planned and executed this well.

She disconnected the IV. Not much else to do than to tell Uncle George the bad news and take him to see Jeremy, Mickey, and Bridget. She walked around a bit to regain her balance, then exited the Eagle and knocked on Uncle George's cabin.

The door opened and Uncle George smiled at her, but quickly it dropped to a frown. "Are they . . ."

Natalie shook her head. "Not yet, as far as I know. But they've been hurt badly. They're in a hospital in Chicago with radiation burns." Natalie dived into Uncle George's bosom and wrapped her arms around his chest. Fresh tears welled up. "I'm so sorry. I tried to save them. I tried to close the wormhole, but I failed! I failed! I failed everyone!"

She sobbed as he patted her on the back. After a couple of minutes, Uncle George said, "I should go see them."

Natalie pulled back and wiped her eyes. "Fastest if we take the Eagle. But if you don't mind me hauling you into the air, I can fly you there as Starlight just as quick, and we won't have to worry about parking."

He patted her on the back. "Fly me there as Starlight, then."

"Be right back." She jogged back to the ship and to her cabin. She reinserted the IV and slipped her mask back on. Once lying in her bed, she said, "Suit, appear here as Starlight." After the change, she picked up Uncle George and headed for Chicago.

Natalie, dressed as herself, and Uncle George stood before Jeremy and Bridget's beds. The pair slept. The doctor beside them checked the readings on the equipment and felt their bodies at key spots. The doctor shook his head. "I don't understand it."

"What?" Natalie blurted out.

Uncle George held up a hand. "How bad is it, doctor?"

"Better than I would have expected when they came in. For whatever reason, they are healing at an accelerated rate."

Natalie stared closely at Jeremy's face. It did appear less red than at first. "Did you sedate them? Can I talk to him?"

The doctor focused on the pair. "That's the odd thing. Shortly after they arrived, they sank into some kind of coma. We've not been able to determine why or what caused it. And before you ask, no, I have no idea when or even if they will come out of it. Physically they are doing well and recovering. But we'll have to see how this coma plays out."

Natalie nodded while she stared at Jeremy.

Uncle George shook the doctor's hand. "Thanks, Doc."

The doctor headed toward the door. "Call if you need anything or have any more questions." He shut the door behind him.

Natalie sat beside Jeremy's bed. The gentle rising of his stomach reminded her at least he still lived. She would be happy if he awoke, but fearful as well. She didn't look forward to telling him the news that not only had she failed, but so had Jornash, and ESEL had succeeded with no seeming way to stop them.

Yet, there was one last option. She could break into their headquarters again. Avoid getting zapped with that virtual stun gun, and find a way to shut it down from there. A long shot? Yes. But what other options were left? And when . . . if Jeremy woke up, she didn't want to face him knowing she hadn't done everything she could. Even if in this case, it mean she'd likely be caught again and have a harder time escaping.

"Uncle." Natalie turned toward him.

He appeared deep in thought. He shook his head. "Uh, yes?"

"I'm going to attack ESEL headquarters. It is the only option left to stop them."

"What will you do?"

She shrugged. "I'm not sure yet. But there is a room where the soldiers' bodies are kept while in the virtual world. If I can figure it out, perhaps there is some way I can turn it all off, unplug it, or something. Won't know till I get there."

He patted her on the back. "Be careful."

She patted his arm. "I'll do my best, which hasn't been enough lately." She grabbed some paper. "Just in case, let me give you the coordinates of the headquarters. If they should happen to wake up, and use their masks, I'm sure I could use the help." She scribbled the numbers on the paper. She paused, then wrote, "Jeremy, I'm sorry I hurt you. I hope what I'm doing today, you'll think better of me. I love you." She signed her name and gave it to Uncle George.

She bent over Jeremy's bed and kissed his lips.

Uncle George hugged her after she left Jeremy's side. "I'll stay here until they throw me out."

She squeezed him back, then exited the room without saying another word. She stepped down the hospital hallways and out into the daylight of a cloudless day. She moved to a grassy area by the side of the building, out of traffic. This was it. Do or die. She'd either come out the hero or virtually die trying.

She straightened her back and entered the coordinates just outside the control room at ESEL headquarters. "Suit, appear at coordinates as Sensei." The hospital lawn faded, and the room of cylinders containing soldiers with Mind Game helmets on filled her view. She immediately dropped into slow-mo to access the situation.

The control room only had two people watching over the place, but she could see a surprised expression slowly forming on one face, and a light on the control panel lit up red. It dawned on her they likely had some way of detecting any virtual bodies in their building. That meant she wouldn't have long. And it explained why they were ready for her when she entered the control room last time.

If she stayed where the soldiers in the Mind Game lay, they might not be able to use their virtual dampening field without disrupting their Zori mission.

She found a place among the cylinders to hide before slow-mo kicked off. The two people in the control room flipped switches and talked on the com, though Natalie couldn't hear what they were saying. She scanned the room for signs of anything she could use to turn the Mind Game helmets off. Aside from a few extra helmets hanging on wall hooks, she didn't spot anything. But she knew that an off-switch wasn't likely unless ESEL had added one, as the Mind Game helmets were self-powered. The only on-off switch was the person in each helmet. Maybe a gravity field in the room, a big black hole, would disrupt the game? It was worth a try.

A soldier entered the room, taking in every detail. "Alright. We know you are here. A virtual dampening field has been initiated around this room. Any attempt to exit will not work. If you surrender, we'll forgo the virtual stun gun."

He said it would prevent her from exiting, but didn't say anything about changing or using her powers. "Suit, appear here as Black Hole." The room faded out, then back in. She checked and her outfit had changed.

"Give up now. We'll soon have a mess of people in here scouring the room. Make it easy on yourself."

Natalie stood up. "Over here, soldier."

He jerked around and pointed the gun at her. "Easy now. No sudden moves. How's about we make a deal?"

Natalie raised an eyebrow. "What kind of deal?"

"You may not be aware, but your friends are dead."

Natalie suppressed a smile. "I know of their fate. That's one reason I'm here."

"There is no need for us to lose the last one of your kind. You can help Earth's defenses. We already control Zori. There is nothing left for you to fight for. It's over."

"So what you are saying is I'm all alone, the cause is lost, and I might as well give up and help you folks. Is that it?"

He nodded. "In a nutshell, yes. Someone with your abilities could go far in our organization. You could have a very nice life."

A nice life. That's all she'd ever wanted and something she'd rarely had. If he spoke the truth, it did sound enticing. "Define, 'nice life.'"

"A high position in the force, maybe in time assistant to Commander Fisher. Personal body guard even. You'd live in luxury, eat full meals, and have pretty much anything you want, within the goals of the organization."

The promises did sound good. But that's all they were, promises. What reason did she have to believe they would keep them? They feared her too much to let her run free in their organization.

She grinned. "You know, I've been alone most of my life. I'm used to playing the rebel. So I'll have to pass on your offer. But thanks anyway."

He fired, and she released two mini-black holes in front of her. The electrical pulses condensed into the black holes and disappeared. A kick from behind her hit her in the small of the back, shoving her into the rows of Mind Game helmets lining the wall. They cascaded around her as she collapsed onto the floor with a thud, each helmet bouncing multiple times in various deep pitches.

The man stood over her with a gun pointed at her. "I've got her, sir."

Natalie smiled through the pain. Did he break something? "You do know bullets won't kill me, right?" She angled her palms toward him and shot a repulsing gravity ray at him. The ray lifted the soldier off his feet and sent him flying through the air. He hit the far wall. She angled another in the general direction of the soldier with the stun gun and blasted. One of the cylinders tore from its hinges and landed several feet away with a chill-bump generating noise.

Natalie tried to get up, but pain shot through her back. She heard movement, as if the first soldier knocked away debris to rise to his feet. What could she do? It was now or never. She extended her hands toward the rows of cylinders.

Then a thought fluttered its way into her mind. If she entered the Mind Game blasting her black holes, her virtual feed would enter the wormhole, possibly collapsing it. But could a virtual body enter another virtual reality? Worth a try. She'd at least take out the players here.

She picked up one of the Mind Game helmets laying next to her and slid it on. She flung her hands outward as the soldier's head popped out from behind a cylinder, the nozzle of the gun leading the way.

She threw out two of the biggest black holes she could muster. "Activate Mind Game!" The needle stung the back of her neck and then darkness flooded over her. The darkness lasted longer than any she recalled from either the Mind Game or the superhero mask.

When her vision returned, she expected to find the ceiling of her cabin, but instead an unfamiliar surface greeted her. She couldn't turn her head. She tried to talk, but her mouth was full of cloth and tied down tight. She could make no sound. No way to reactivate her superheroes.

A man's face leaned into view. Commander Fisher!

He smiled. "Back from playing superhero, I see." He yanked the mask off her head. "We'll have no more of this for now. At least until we come to an understanding."

Natalie heard the sound of jet engines. The slight turbulence at one point confirmed they rode in an aircraft.

"An understanding that says you are mine. Body and all." He smirked. "Oh yes, I'm sure you're wondering how we found your body. Carelessness on your part, actually. We saw you fly away in a silver outfit, apparently carrying your Uncle George. Just took a little exploring to find the cloaked ship and your body in it."

He sat back. "Welcome to ESEL, Natalie. Whether you like it or not."

She knew she didn't like it. Question was, did she collapse the wormhole?

Chapter 17

Jeremy batted his eyes open. He jerked up but quickly fell back onto a pillow. Memory returned. They'd been taken to a hospital. Natalie flew off to collapse the wormhole. She'd saved them from ESEL's death trap. Apparently successfully since he was still alive. He bent his head to find Uncle George in a chair, his chin on his chest, snoring away.

The door to the room flung open and two nurses, followed by a doctor, poured into the area. One nurse checked Jeremy's readings while the other checked on Bridget, who groaned. Uncle George jerked awake and stood on his feet. A smile spread across his face.

The doctor rechecked the nurses' readings. "Amazing."

Jeremy glanced at him and the nurse. "What?"

"That you're doing as well as you are. When you came in here, it appeared you'd been badly burnt by radiation. Now it's like you only have a bad sunburn. Any idea why?"

Jeremy shrugged. "I could guess, but no real explanation that makes any sense. How long have we been out?"

"Almost two days." The doctor shook his head. "I've never seen burn victims recover so fast. This amount of healing takes months, not hours. You'd think these folk were from Mars or something."

The nurse did a double-take. "Doctor, I can assure you they are human."

He laughed. "I know, I know. I've seen the x-rays and scans. But I don't have any other answer." He headed toward the door. "I'll go check out your friend in the other room. If he's as far advanced as you two are, I can sign the release papers." He disappeared behind the closing door.

Uncle George stood at the edge of Jeremy's bed as the nurse removed the monitoring electrodes and other connections. "I'm so glad you're okay." His face dropped. "I do have some bad news, however."

Jeremy froze. "She's not dead, is she?"

Uncle George shook his head. "Not that I know of, yet. She couldn't collapse the wormhole. Something about a virtual dampening field surrounding it. She couldn't figure a way to get past it. So she gave up and returned to my cabin. That's when she carried me here."

Jeremy rose to a sitting position and swung his feet over the side of the bed. "So, where is Natalie? In Mickey's room?" Heat rose to his face at the thought of them together again.

"No." Uncle George handed Jeremy a piece of paper. "She wanted me to give this to you."

Jeremy read the note. She listed coordinates to ESEL headquarters, and a note. Jeremy batted back water attempting to escape. "What does she mean, she hopes I'll think better of her after today?"

Uncle George cleared his throat. "She went to ESEL headquarters to see if she could stop them. Said something about that's where the soldiers are plugged into the Mind Game."

Jeremy pushed himself off the bed. "How long ago?"

"Yeah, we need to help her!" Bridget landed on her feet, and wobbled a moment before stabilizing.

"About six hours, and I've not heard from her since."

Jeremy searched the area. "Where's my mask?"

Uncle George pointed at the table next to the bed. "I believe they stored your personal belongings in the drawer there."

Jeremy pulled the drawer open and rifled through the items. He pulled out his mask.

Bridget said, "I've got mine."

Jeremy pulled his over his head and laid back down. "Uncle, I know this will be hard to explain to them, but do your best."

He sighed. "Will do."

"Suit, appear here as Astro Man." Nothing happened.

Bridget yelled out, "Suit, appear here as Comet Girl." No Comet Girl appeared by her bed.

The door opened and Mickey rushed in. "The mask, it doesn't work. Natalie must have collapsed the wormhole!"

Jeremy held up a hand. "No, she didn't. At least that's what she told Uncle George. So Jornash must have shut down the virtual machine." Jeremy imagined a barren world on Zori, with only blobs of goo lying across the landscape where cities used to be.

"Oh, I forgot," Uncle George said. "She also told me when she was attempting to get past the dampening field around the wormhole, she received a message from Jornash. If I recall correctly . . ." He stared at the ceiling and rubbed his beard. "ESEL had broken through their defenses and taken over their building, including the virtual machine. But, he did say he locked them out of it, so it will take a while for them to hack into it and learn its secrets."

Jeremy's heart sank. "If our virtual heroes don't work anymore, she must have been successful at shutting it all down. But what happened to her? And now we don't have any way to find out or help her if she needs help."

No one said anything for a minute. A cart rattled down the hall; he glanced in its direction. A woman pushed a lunch cart on the other side of the wall. His thoughts returned to Natalie.

Jeremy jerked his head up. "I just saw the woman pushing the lunch cart."

Mickey wrinkled his brow. "Bucko, so did I when she passed by the door. I forgot to close it."

"No, no. I saw her on the other side of the wall, before she reached the door. I saw through the wall, Mick. Just like Astro Man."

Mickey's stare bored into Jeremy while his mind connected the dots. He extended his hands and he floated into the air. "I'm flying, like G Man."

Bridget leaped into the air, her hospital gown flapping in the air as she left a trail of sparkling dust in her wake. "And I can fly like Comet Girl!"

Jeremy watched them both floating though the air. "I know this is going to sound so like a typical superhero origin story, but I can't think of any other explanation. It appears the radiation from that nuclear blast fused the abilities of the virtual superheroes we were at the time into our real bodies."

Mickey stared at his hands as his head floated inches from the ceiling. "You mean, now I am G Man?"

"And I'm always going to be Comet Girl?"

"Well, Sis. Who knows how long this will last, but it appears so for the moment. So, likewise, I'm now Astro Man." The thought was both exciting and sad at the same time. Exciting, because now it was no longer virtual power, but he would put his own life on the line to help people. That could make him less confident. But it also meant ESEL couldn't steal his body, or take over his powers.

Jeremy reached for his pants in the small closet next to his bed. "Let's check out of this joint and see if we can find Natalie."

———

A soldier entered the room and saluted. "Sir, we have a situation."

The commander stood and answered the salute. "At ease, soldier."

Natalie watched as Commander Fisher moved to the soldier and whispered with him. At one point the commander cried out, "That's impossible!" His face grew very grim, his eyes burned with hate. She was sure she'd end up the one he took his anger out on. Whatever news he had received, it was not good.

The commander sat back by Natalie. He removed the gag from her mouth. "No longer a need for that." He forced a smile that didn't want to be there. "Now, I don't suppose you'd know anything about the disappearance of an island lately. Hum?"

Natalie swallowed. Did she create a black hole big enough to swallow an island? But she didn't want to let on if he didn't know for sure it was her doing. "How could I do that?"

"I'm sure it would be easy enough for a superhero to find a nuclear bomb and drop it on an island."

She jerked up. "Nuclear bomb? I don't know anything about that." If they had nuclear bombs on site, it is possible that the compression and heat generated by spaghettification could have triggered them. They must have had some in an adjoining room because the black hole effect would have vanished with her entry into the Mind Game, so it shouldn't have had enough time to suck in a lot of the area other than the immediate building. The thought caused her to wonder if her stunt had collapsed the wormhole or not. At least if she had inadvertently destroyed the island, the invading force on Zori had been neutralized. But it wouldn't stop them from trying again and again. But perhaps by then, they could find a way to collapse the wormhole.

If the wormhole was still operational, Jeremy, Mickey, and Bridget could be along in due time to save her. Or if she could get that mask back. Fat chance on that score. But if she had been successful in taking out the wormhole, there was no one to save her. Once ESEL learned it was gone, so was her usefulness. With no superheroes to save her, she knew the end would be death.

"Miss Shinhaw," the commander bored into her eyes. "I don't have time for games. You should know that we left troops at your Uncle George's cabin. When he returns, if you have not been cooperative, we will not be treating him very nicely. It could even result in his death, as regretful as that would be.

"So, tell me, do you know anything about what happened on that island?"

Natalie stared at the ceiling, the only direction she could stare. "I don't know anything."

Commander Fisher sucked in a deep breath. "Very well. We'll do this the hard way. When we arrive at our destination, expect some rather intense interrogation. If you wish to avoid that option, just let me know." He stared at her for a moment before standing and leaving the room.

Pressure sores ached on her shoulders and rear. She wanted to move, but they had her tied down so tightly she could barely twitch her nose. Well, she knew this was one likely outcome. She shouldn't be surprised. The ironic thing was if she'd successfully collapsed the wormhole, it pretty much ensured she would die. At least Jeremy, Mickey, and Bridget should be able to live normal lives again. "I love you, Jeremy."

Chapter 18

Jeremy kept thinking about the surreal scene. They flew through the sky in their normal clothes. Bridget's hair flapped against the wind as comet dust followed in her wake. Mickey flew alongside Jeremy, who because of Astro Man's gravity ray on his gun, was able to duplicate Mickey's G Man levitation. Mickey kept a gravity ray on Uncle George who flew underneath him. And they weren't virtual, which also meant they couldn't turn it off either. Nor did they have a space station on Titan to use as a base.

The ground sped under them. Within fifteen minutes, they'd traversed the distance from Chicago to Uncle George's hidden cabin. As they approached, Mickey stopped and put his hand out.

Bridget circled back and halted in front of them. "What's up?"

Mickey pointed toward the area where Uncle George's cabin rested. "Do you see what I do?"

Jeremy focused until he spotted the cabin. A small helicopter rested behind it. "Uncle? Do you know who's helicopter that is?"

He ran his fingers through his beard. "Nope. And it's sitting right where Natalie's invisible space ship stood."

Jeremy pointed at a ledge several feet to the south and up from the cabin. "How about we put Uncle there and let's check out the situation."

Mickey nodded. "Sounds good to me. Maybe we can get some information on Natalie." Mickey flew to the ledge and deposited Uncle George on it. "Be back in a jiffy." He returned to the other two. "Now, what's the plan?"

Jeremy rubbed his chin. "Bridget, you fly over the helicopter and make it not work, and over the house to disrupt any communication devices. Mickey and I will deal with anyone we find." Jeremy paused. "And remember, we're not virtual anymore. We can die, despite our superpowers. So be careful."

They both nodded. Bridget flew on ahead. Mickey and Jeremy followed behind her, but dropped low to come at the house from underneath the ledge. Bridget flew in circles over the house and helicopter, covering them with comet dust.

"Okay, let's move in, Mick." Jeremy shifted to x-ray vision and scanned the cabin. Five men waited inside, though they didn't appear to be aware they were about to be blindsided. "There are five inside with guns, but they don't know we're here. I'll take two, and you handle the other three with your gravity ray. Make them so heavy they can't get up."

Mickey patted Jeremy on the back. "Good idea. That way we can interrogate them."

They both flew fast into the door, shattering it to pieces. The five men jumped as the pair skidded to a halt. They went for their guns. Jeremy lifted his hands and shot two gravity rays at the left two, while Mickey used both hands, cupped together, to make a broad gravity ray enveloping the other three. They all sank to the floor, their guns fell to their sides as if 300 pound weights were attached to each one.

They both kept their beams trained on the five as they walked toward them. Jeremy stood over one of them. "Where did they take the girl?"

The soldier stoically stared at the ceiling.

Jeremy focused his ray beam on the man's left hand holding his gun, and then switched to the ice ray for a second, encasing his hand in inch-thick ice. "Where did they take the girl?"

The man lay tight-lipped on the floor. His chin quivered.

Jeremy encased his arm up to his elbow in ice. "Where?"

The soldier shivered and gritted his teeth, but refused to talk.

Jeremy iced the rest of his arm. "We could do this all day."

The soldier squeezed his eyes shut and clenched his teeth. "And I would enjoy it."

Jeremy glanced at Mickey. His eyes said what he thought. These guys were probably trained to endure all sorts of torture. He could do this all day and not get anywhere. Every lost minute might be a minute too late to save Natalie.

Jeremy changed the rays to stun, and his two men's eyes closed. He then trained his ray on the other three Mickey held and knocked them out cold. Mickey turned off his gravity ray.

Mickey kicked one of the men's legs. "How long does your stun last?"

"If it mimics Astro Man's, then about four to five hours." Jeremy snapped his fingers and pulled a piece of paper from his pocket. "Natalie gave me the coordinates to their headquarters. That should be the first place to check."

Mickey smiled. They stepped outside where Bridget sat on a bench.

She uncrossed her arms. "About time. What took so long?"

Jeremy pointed his right thumb back at the

cabin. "An unsuccessful interrogation. We decided we didn't need their help and stunned them. Mick, you go get Uncle George and bring him here. Bridget and I will go to Uncle George's house to make sure it's clear. We'll meet back here."

Mickey saluted and shot into the sky. Jeremy and Bridget leaped off the edge of the mountain and sailed across to Uncle George's house.

As he approached, Jeremy switched to x-ray vision and searched for any sign of ESEL occupation. He could find none. "Bridget, I think they've abandoned Uncle George's house. But just in case, blanket the house with "no communication" dust. Once they found Natalie, I guess they had no reason to keep surveillance on Uncle George's house, just his cabin."

She flew over the house three times, releasing comet dust. Once she finished, they flew back to Uncle George's cabin where Mickey and Uncle George waited for them.

Jeremy landed. "Uncle, do you have any friends you could stay with in town for a day or two?"

Uncle George pulled on his beard. "I suppose Jack would let me stay with him. Not sure if on such short notice. But we could check."

Jeremy rubbed his hands together. "Okay, here's the plan. We'll take these five men to the city jail. Uncle George can file charges of breaking and entering. That should tie them up for a while after they wake up. Then, we'll take Uncle George to his friend's house. After that, we take a trip to the library so we can use their computers to the coordinates to their headquarters that Natalie gave me. Then we're on our way to find Natalie and hopefully reach her in time, if it's not already too late. Got it?"

Everyone nodded.

"Then let's get to it." *And who knows, maybe we can shut down ESEL in the process, for good.*

———

One soldier stood over her with a rifle while the other handcuffed her before releasing the straps that had bound her to the bed. She rejoiced in finally moving again after several hours of being forced to lie in one position. But she didn't look forward to what lay ahead.

The door opened and Commander Fisher entered. "Is the prisoner ready?"

They both saluted. "Yes, sir."

"Then follow me." He turned and exited. The soldiers pushed Natalie to follow. They left the jet and crossed the small air field. Tropical vegetation surrounded them, so they were likely still in the Pacific somewhere. But the compound wasn't as big as the main headquarters had been. Fewer and smaller buildings.

They entered a gate. Soldiers worked here and there. Some glanced at her as they headed to the biggest building in the area. As they entered, a soldier met Commander Fisher and saluted. Natalie struggled to hear what they said, but they whispered.

Then Commander Fisher's mouth frowned, his teeth clenched, and his face reddened. "How could that have happened?"

The soldier winced, but continued in a soft tone.

"I had ordered all measures taken to protect that worm . . ." Commander Fisher returned to whispering, but from his tense facial expressions, no less strongly.

The commander turned to the soldiers holding Natalie. "Put her in a cell for now, until I can sort through recent events."

The soldiers saluted. "Yes, sir."

The commander led the soldier he'd been

talking with down one hall while the two guarding her directed her feet down a different hallway. They stopped at a cell door, opened it, and put her in it after undoing her cuffs.

Natalie watched them leave. A guard stood at both ends of the hallway. The cell contained a makeshift bench, a toilet, and a sink. A thin blanket lay across the bench. She guessed that was her bed. She sat on the bench, thankful to be able to move and stretch.

Obviously, Commander Fisher had received news that the wormhole had collapsed. She wished she could do a happy dance right there in the cell, but she knew they likely had cameras trained on her, so she repressed even a smile. But Jeremy could finally live a normal life. He could go find a girl that would treat him better than she had. Because now there was no hope of anyone coming to her rescue.

Her only hope lay in avoiding blame for the wormhole collapse. Commander Fisher might release her since she could no longer do any damage. She couldn't become a superhero any longer, short-lived as the career was. But she knew release wasn't likely. She knew too much about the secret organization. They'd not likely let her run around the country with that knowledge.

Nope, the next step for Commander Fisher was to put her out of her misery. She was of no use to him anymore and too much of a risk to let go. But he might try to extract more information out of her before he did that. Maybe she could use that in some way.

Natalie let a small smile crack through. She'd earned that. *I won. ESEL lost. Take that, you power-hungry snakes!* She could die at least knowing she'd done one deed worthy of a hero.

Jeremy stopped and hovered over the ocean waves rolling beneath him. "We're here, but where is the island?"

Bridget pulled to a stop beside him. "Maybe it's cloaked."

Mickey laughed. "I don't think anyone on Earth has that level of cloaking technology."

Bridget crossed her arms. "I saw it on TV one time."

"But that's just small objects. That couldn't work on a whole island."

She huffed. "You think they're going to tell you everything they've developed?"

Jeremy waved a hand at them. "Okay, okay. I've checked the area with every type of vision Astro Man has. I don't see an island, but my infrared vision does pick up radiation particles. On the scale of a major nuclear explosion."

"Nuclear?" Mickey shook his head. That doesn't sound good. What if Natalie—"

"We can't assume that yet." Jeremy rubbed his forehead. "Bridget, time to use your find dust. It will tell us if Natalie is no more or somewhere else."

Bridget extended her arms. "Go find Natalie!" Comet dust raced from her fingertips. It gathered into a ten-foot ball a little ways away and hovered. Jeremy glanced at Mickey. Worry covered his face. Then the dust headed across the waters toward the horizon.

Jeremy let out a breath he'd been holding. She wasn't dead. "Come on guys. Follow that dust."

Chapter 19

One soldier opened the cell door while another kept a gun pointed at Natalie. "Follow me."

Natalie fell into step behind him while the gun-toting soldier kept his muzzle in her back. She prayed he had a steady finger. They traveled across five different halls before entering a room. The equivalent of a dentist chair lay in the center, and the back wall supported a row of the same cylinders she saw at headquarters, but only one contained a body. Had the wormhole been destroyed?

They forced her down upon a table and strapped her in.

Commander Fisher grinned as he focused on her. "Miss Shinhaw, I'll ask you one last time, do you know anything about the destruction of an island in the Pacific?"

"No more than I knew last time you asked me that question."

"Do you have any information or knowledge about an attack on the wormhole leading to Zori?"

Natalie feigned surprise. "Oh my, you mean the wormhole has been attacked? Who would do such a dastardly thing?"

"Miss Shinhaw, if you tell me now, I won't have to resort to the most unpleasant task of sending you into another world that you won't like."

Natalie stared straight ahead and remained silent.

The commander slammed his fist on the bed and forced his face less than an inch away from Natalie's. "Very well. You are about to enter a hostile world, laden with predators. To escape, all you need to do is find a telephone, and dial 911. Then tell the operator the answers to the two questions I just asked you. You will stay in this world as long as necessary. Do you understand?"

Natalie grunted. "Whatever."

A helmet slid over her head. From what she saw of it, it appeared to be a Mind Game helmet.

"Helmet in position," one man said.

"Activating Virtual Game."

Virtual Game? A needle plunged into the back of her neck. The room disappeared into darkness.

As the light returned, she stood in a wooden framed building. The room lay bare save for a couch and coffee table. Stain color covered the walls. But in the center of the room stood an end table with an old-fashioned dial phone on it.

Should she leave or stay? The correlation to an old movie gave her the creeps. Shades of Rillian all over again. The phone rang over and over again. She figured it wasn't going to stop until she answered it.

She stepped toward it and lifted the receiver. "Miss Shinhaw, if you are not going to answer the questions, I'd suggest you start running. Good luck." A dial tone replaced the voice.

Run? She could only see one door. She ran and opened it. A spiral staircase wound beneath her, but a beast jogged its way up it no more than two stories down. No doubt this was what she should be running from. She didn't want to wait and find out.

She closed the door and locked it, then

sped to a window, opened it, and looked out. A thin ledge stood many stories from the ground. A busy street lay below, and other skyscrapers filled the horizon. *Why is there always a ledge, and its always thin?*

She craned her neck to see an empty window washer's cart hanging by ropes a few feet away. "That's not happening. It's an invitation to disaster." She scanned the room. An air duct grating sat close to the floor on one wall. She was thin, she could likely fit. But she really didn't have enough time to take the screws off and get in before the monster arrived.

She screamed at the ceiling, "I'm not going to play this game!"

The door crashed in and a hulk of what appeared to be an orc stood before her. It growled and bared its fangs before lunging at her. She raised her hands before its teeth sank into her flesh. It tore at her, ripping into her arms and legs. It's claws shredded her flesh. Each strike radiated pain like the first.

She screamed in agony until either due to loss of blood or the destruction of a vital organs, her vision dimmed into blackness. When light returned, she stood in the same room as before, shaking from the trauma she had just endured.

The phone rang. She picked it up. "Are you ready to answer the questions? Or will you run this time?" Commander Fisher laughed.

She slammed the phone down. She could hear the monster running up the stairs. She glanced at the air duct, ran to it, and yanked until the screws dislodged from the dry wall. She flung the vent cover aside and dove in as the monster crashed in the door. She scurried up the vent but the monster ripped apart the wall until it grabbed her kicking feet and yanked her out. Then the eating began anew, leaving Natalie screaming into the void.

The comet dust arced its way downward toward a small island in the Pacific ocean, then vanished as if to say, "We're here."

Jeremy pointed at the lone set of buildings on the island. "Put up your shields, there's nothing to do but go in with guns blazing. Bridget, flash some lights going in, but warn us first. Then scatter not-working dust over any guns and weapons you see. Mick and I will keep them busy with explosions and such."

Bridget shot toward the compound, creating a shield with her comet dust as she flew. Jeremy and Mickey followed behind her. As Jeremy expected, it didn't take long before mortar fire shot up toward them. One blasted against his shield. Jeremy extended a hand and fired a ray at the weapons, which exploded into a ball of flames. Soldiers ran from the site. Mickey shot gravity rays at the canons causing them to crumble into a mess of metal.

"Here I go!" Bridget announced as she dived toward the compound like a bomber on a run.

Jeremy and Mickey closed their eyes. Light flashed behind his closed eyelids.

"Okay, you can open them now."

Jeremy peered at the compound. All weapons had ceased firing. Soldiers staggered around with their hands over their eyes.

Bridget cascaded comet dust over the area. Guns and communication devices would now fail to work.

Jeremy and Mickey landed on the ground just outside a building he guessed was the main office. A group of soldiers, eyes still blinking, surged toward them. Some tried to fire their guns, but nothing happened.

Mickey laid a hand on Jeremy's shoulder. "Rise into the air a bit and let me handle this."

Jeremy did as Mickey instructed. The soldiers raced toward them, closing fast. Mickey held his arms straight out from his body and started spinning. A ray shot from both hands. Anything they hit floated into the air if it were not attached to the ground. The soldiers' feet left the earth, and they floated several feet into the air before plummeting back to the dirt with a loud thump.

Jeremy landed, and Bridget settled to the ground beside him. Jeremy opened the door to the building. Five soldiers stood ready with guns. Mickey threw up a gravity shield. The bullets repelled from the shield as if they hit metal. Jeremy dropped each man with his stun ray. He shifted to x-ray vision to search for Natalie. After a minute, he spotted her in a cylinder. *What was she doing in there if the wormhole had been destroyed?* "This way. There are three more men around this next corner."

They worked their way down the halls. For each group of soldiers they encountered, Bridget blinded them, and Jeremy fired his stun rays from behind Mickey's shields. When they arrived at the room containing Natalie, they discovered a locked door.

Mickey said, "Stand back." He pointed a hand at the door and shot a ray at it. The door dissolved into a puddle of liquid in a matter of seconds.

They entered the room. Several cylinders lined the back wall of the control room. Some Mind Game helmets hung from another wall. Computer equipment covered the walls on the opposite side. One screen caught Jeremy's attention. A monster attacked Natalie, ripping her apart.

Jeremy heard a click. He swirled around

and threw up a shield. Commander Fisher fired a pistol. The bullet ricocheted off Jeremy's shield and hit Bridget in the chest. She crumbled to the ground.

Commander Fisher smiled. "Well, well. What do we have here? Looks like maybe the wormhole isn't closed after all. Another one, perhaps?"

Jeremy clenched his teeth. "In your dreams." He fired a stun ray and Commander Fisher dropped to the floor in a heap.

Jeremy rushed to Bridget. She stared up at him. "I'm shot."

He patted her on the shoulder. "You'll be alright. Just hold on." He turned to Mickey. "Can you get her to a hospital?"

"You bet. But you'll be alone."

"I don't see we have much option at this point. It's either let my sister bleed to death or leave Natalie here." He scanned the controls. "Here's an exit button. I should be able to get her out. You go on with Bridget."

He nodded, wrapped Bridget in a weightless field, and headed out the door with her.

Soldiers yelled and gunfire sounded, then silence. Jeremy turned his attention to the monitor. Natalie stood in the room again. "This is replaying over and over. She's reliving being eaten alive." The room didn't look like anything on Zori. It dawned on him that ESEL must have advanced to the point of creating their own immersive virtual reality using the Mind Game helmets. They needed the technology of the Stuians to take it to the next level, interacting with reality like Zori's virtual world did.

Thanks to Natalie, they didn't get that far. She had sacrificed herself to collapse the wormhole. She didn't know they had retained their super powers. She wouldn't be expecting to be saved.

Jeremy pushed the exit button. The phone started ringing in the virtual world. Natalie yelled, "I told you, I'm not playing your game!"

"No, Natalie. Pick up the phone!" For whatever reason, she had to pick up the phone to exit. The phone continued to ring as the beast burst through the door and attacked her again. Jeremy averted his eyes. He couldn't stomach the bloody scene. After a few seconds, he checked the monitor. Blackness covered it, but it flickered to life, and Natalie stood in the room again. Jeremy hit the exit button. The phone rang.

Natalie threw up her hands and yelled. "Okay, you win! I don't know why you want to know this stupid information anyway." She yanked the phone up and put it to her ear. "I was at your headquarters as Black Hole, a virtual superhero created by the Stuians. I put on a Mind Game helmet, and started two big black holes. By using the Mind Game feed, it took my virtual body and black holes into the wormhole, bypassing your lame damping field, collapsing the worm hole, and at the same time, the black holes I formed before going into the Mind Game must have detonated nuclear explosives you had on site. Bad idea by the way. That's why your precious little headquarters island blew up. Now, get me out of here so you can kill me proper like."

"Brilliant!"

"What? Who is this?"

The monster broke through the door. The button marked "exit" blinked. He punched it, and Natalie vanished from the room on the monitor. She thrashed about in the cylinder. Jeremy jumped up and disengaged the locks. The liquid drained, and then the locks clicked open, and the lid popped out. Jeremy disconnected Natalie and lifted the helmet from her head. He hugged her. He hadn't lost her. He almost did. He smiled. He didn't want to lose her. He couldn't give her up without a fight.

She stared at him. "Jeremy, what are you doing here?"

"I'll explain later. Right now we need to get you out of here." He helped her out of the cylinder. "But before we leave, we should take care of a little business."

The door to the room flew open and soldiers started filing in, pointing their rifles at them. Jeremy held up a hand and projected a shield toward them. The bullets bounced off it. The shield rammed into them, sending them cascading back into one another. While they lay on the floor, Jeremy shot stun rays, knocking them all asleep.

Natalie's eyes squinted at him. "How can you do that with the wormhole collapsed?"

"I'll explain later." Jeremy blasted his ray around the room, destroying computers, helmets, and the cylinders. "They probably have more of these locations, but might as well take out one while we're here."

Then Jeremy pointed his hand at the ceiling as equipment burned around him, and blasted a hole to a clear sky. "Up, up, and away!" He leaped up with her in his arms and they sailed through the hole. He glanced at Natalie in his arms as they soared through the clouds. She grinned at him.

He smiled back. "Sorry, but I've always wanted to say that."

Chapter 20

The doctor flipped through Bridget's chart and shook his head. "What are you kids into? First radiation burns, now gun shots?" Bridget had returned from surgery and lay groggily in a hospital bed.

Mickey laughed. "Doc, surely you see plenty of gun shot wounds in Chicago."

He flipped another page. "You're right there. But I've never seen a partially dissolved bullet. It was as if the body was healing itself. What we pulled out in surgery didn't resemble any bullet I've ever seen."

Jeremy shrugged. "My family comes from a long line of quick healers."

The doctor squinted at him. "Where are you from?"

"Montana."

He grunted. "That explains it. She'll be fine in a day or two, though with how quickly you all healed from your radiation burns, I'd guess she might be dismissed by the end of the day. I'll be back to check on her." He stepped out of the room.

Uncle George seated himself in a chair. Mickey had picked him up after dropping Bridget off.

Jeremy patted Mickey's back. "Thanks for all you did."

He waved his hand. "Tis nothing."

Jeremy glanced at Natalie. "Mick, I'll be back in a bit." Jeremy took Natalie's hand and led her outside the hospital to a bench in a grassy area and sat down. He stared at the birds flying through the air for a few seconds. "Natalie, I'm not sure—"

"I know, I know." She held up a hand. "I don't deserve a second chance. What I did was wrong. I lied to you. I lied to Mickey. I lied to myself. You're better off without me."

Jeremy stared at her. He breathed deep. "As I was going to say, I'm not sure I can go on without you."

She smiled, but it faded. "You don't know all about me. I survived on the streets using my smarts, yes. But I also survived by lying and stealing. I had to fight for me because no one else did. Take advantage of others or they'd take advantage of you. It turned me into a very selfish person. A person who doesn't deserve happiness or most of all, you. It is best for both you and Mickey if I return to the streets. That is where I belong. Then I won't be a distraction."

"Natalie . . ." Jeremy bowed his head. "You can change with the right help." He lifted his head and met her eyes. "But you've got to want it. I believe you are more than a cheater. You deserve a better life. But it won't happen unless you give it all you've got."

Her eyes watered up. "Oh, Jeremy. I don't want to hurt you again." Her head fell onto his shoulders. "If I love you, I should let you go."

"Natalie. How much do you love me?"

She lifted her head, wiped her eyes and stared at Jeremy. "I love you with all my heart. I'd do anything for you, including staying away from you."

"How about being willing to go to some intensive counseling, read books, seek spiritual help, learn about yourself, and make the changes to become a better person? Whatever it takes. Do you love me enough to do that?"

She stared at the ground for a few seconds before meeting his eyes. "Yes."

"Then let me take that risk. I honestly didn't know if I could be with you going forward. It may be if you blow it again, it will end things. But if there is a chance to save you, I want to do that. For you. Why? Because I love you that much."

She wrapped her arms around Jeremy's shoulders and squeezed tightly. "Thank you, thank you, thank you so much!"

Tears trickled down his shoulder. His own eyes started watering as well. He blinked it back and squeezed Natalie tighter.

––––––––

Jeremy met each set of eyes in Bridget's hospital room. Bridget sat up in her bed, already acting like herself. Uncle George, Mickey, and Natalie all sat around her bed.

Jeremy cleared his throat. "We three didn't ask for these powers. I was honestly looking forward to living a normal life. But fate hasn't dealt us that hand. Our lives are—"

"Bucko!" Mickey raised a hand. "Really? Cut to the chase, man. You're overdoing the leader-gives-a-speech thing."

Jeremy grinned. "Of course. This time I am over analyzing. Bottom line, ESEL will be after us. We can't stay at Uncle George's house or his cabin. They will be watching those locations." Jeremy focused on Uncle George. "And that means you too, Uncle. They'll use you as bait if they can find you. Is there anywhere else you can go?"

He sighed. "Well, I didn't want to tell anyone."

Mickey laughed. "Don't tell me you have another cabin in the woods."

Uncle George nodded. "I wanted one place I could get away to and no one else would know where to find me. But considering the circumstances, it would make a good hideout. I only request you take extra precautions not to let them find it. I'm all out of cabins."

"How far from your house is it?"

He rubbed his beard. "I'd say about fifty miles, give or take five."

Jeremy smiled. "That should work. It needs to be far enough away from your house that they can't pick up our activity. We'll all need to keep a low profile. Especially Uncle George and Natalie. We have a fighting chance, but you two do not. We don't want to attract ESEL's attention to the hideout."

Mickey raised a hand. "If you want a normal life, why not just live it?"

"Two reasons. One, ESEL knows we have these powers now. We played our hand in saving Natalie. They won't stop just because we do, now that they know we're still active. They probably think we still have some way to be virtual.

"Two, I don't think if I see someone being abused or hurting someone, that I can walk by knowing I could do something about it. Could you?"

Mickey shook his head. "I see your point. But that then leads to this question. Are we going to be career superheroes, or only when we have to be? I mean, are we going to seek out people to save? Will we have costumes and masks to keep our identities secret?"

Jeremy leaned forward. "We will be superheroes. And keeping our identities secret would be a good thing. But I think our first order of business before we go attracting attention saving everyone we can find is to first deal with ESEL. I don't think they are done. Once they are out of the picture, we can think about a more full time superhero career."

Uncle George raised a hand. "I can take care of the costumes. If Natalie will help me."

She smiled. "I'd be glad to help."

Jeremy held his hand out, palm down over the end of Bridget's bed. "Are we in agreement?"

Each person put their hands on top of Jeremy's.

Jeremy smiled. "I dub thee, The Fellowship of Heroes."

Everyone chuckled. Jeremy sat back. "Any questions?"

Bridget raised her hand. "Yeah. When does this fellowship eat? I'm hungry."

Jeremy grinned. "I'm sure we'll have some vittles soon, Sis."

She wrinkled her brow. "Vittles?"

Jeremy's mind returned to Zori. He prayed they would be safe. And it would be a long time before another person came along to become their dictator. They were on their own now, for good or bad. But he would miss them.

Events had once again changed the direction of his life. And he had a feeling it would continue to be that way. If the past two years were any indication, his "normal" would be ever evolving.

He knew they couldn't hear him, but he softly said, as Bridget and Mickey discussed dinner, "Thank you, Rillian, Zorians, Stuians, and ESEL for making me who I am today." He smiled at those around him. "And my friends." He reached out and grabbed Natalie's hand. "Including Natalie. Especially Natalie."

She smiled back at him. They had a long road ahead of them, but he'd taken on so much already, what was one more challenge? He squeezed her hand and she returned the sentiment. They'd make it after all.

About the Author

Personal Note: Thank you for reading *Virtual Game*. As you can tell by the ending, the story is not over. I expected it would be, but alas, sometimes stories take on a life of their own. Or maybe it's just my subconscious not wanting to end the ride. Who knows. But the next novel is in the planning stages. To keep in the loop, be sure to use the links below for my publishing news.

I invite you to leave your honest feedback on Amazon, Barnes and Noble, Kobo, Apple, Goodreads, or any other online retail outlet you frequent.

Plus, if you've skipped reading the first two books in the series—*Mind Game* and *Hero Game*—make sure you grab those to get the full story. Read the free *Virtual Hero* collection of short stories in this world for more fun. For more information, visit http://www.rlcopple.com/.

R. L. Copple's interest in speculative fiction started after reading Runaway Robot by Lester Del Ray in 1970. Many others followed by Asimov, Bradbury, Heinlein, Tolkien, C. S. Lewis. In 2005, he started writing speculative fiction. *Infinite Realities* marks his first book, a

fantasy novella published in November 2007, republished as a full novel in 2012 titled, *Reality's Dawn*. His second book and first novel, *Transforming Realities*, hit the shelves March 2009, also republished in 2012 as *Reality's Ascent*. He has also published *Mind Game*, *Hero Game*, *Ethereal Worlds* anthology, and *How to Make an Ebook: Using Free Software*. He has been published in several magazines.

More info can be found at:

Website: **http://www.rlcopple.com**.

Twitter: **http://www.twitter.com/rlcopple**

Facebook:

http://www.facebook.com/rlcoppleauthor

Blog: **http://blog.rlcopple.com**

Other Novels by R. L. Copple

From Splashdown Books

The Reality Chronicles
Book 1: *Reality's Dawn*
Book 2: *Reality's Ascent*
Book 3: *Reality's Fire*

From Ethereal Press

The Legend of the Dragons' Dying Field
Book 1: *The Magic Within*

The Virtual Chronicles
Book 1: *Mind Game*
Book 2: *Hero Game*
Book 3: *Virtual Game*
Book 4: *Reality Game*

Ethereal Worlds, Vol. 1 & 2
Science Fiction and Fantasy Short Story Anthology

Find more information on these exciting

stories at

http://www.rlcopple.com/

www.ingramcontent.com/pod-product-compliance
Lightning Source LLC
Chambersburg PA
CBHW072050170626
46813CB00004B/1294